THE RISE AND FALL

of the

CYDONIAN STAR EMPIRE

a novel by

RICHARD J. PARACKA

ACKNOWLEDGEMENTS AND PERMISSIONS

National Aeronautics and Space Administration - NASA

For the use of the star field image *NGC6726_Schedler_960*, which was modified for cover art used for this book.

For the use of the image of The Face on Mars at the Cydonia site – discovered July 25, 1976 by the Viking 1 orbiter.

Thunderchild Publishing, Inc.

For the use of the term and description of the Interocitor.

For computer imaging scientists –

Vincent DiPietro and Gregory Molenaar, who discovered The Face, the 5 sided pyramid (named D&M pyramid in their honor) and the city ruins - all in close proximity to The Face.

Dr. John E. Brandenburg, Ph.D. –

For his book DEATH ON MARS, in which he provided mathematical calculations of the size and location of thermonuclear devices used and corroborating evidence for the theory of a nuclear holocaust that may have destroyed the ecosphere of Mars.

For the Lord God Master of the Universe –

Who graciously provided inspiration and motivation, without which this book could not have been written.

THE RISE AND FALL of the CYDONIAN STAR EMPIRE

TABLE OF CONTENTS

Introduction

In June 1976 NASA technicians guided their Viking 1 spacecraft into a stable orbit around the planet Mars. One of its first tasks was to photograph regions of the planet that would be suitable as landing zones for its soil sampler component as well as that of its sister ship Viking 2. During examination of a photographic study of the Cydonia region, a startling discovery was made – a rock formation that resembled a human face.

NASA technicians have always been in the habit of assigning familiar names to astronomical bodies and formations. Future references are eased when familiar terms are used instead of alphanumeric code designations. True to form NASA named the strange stone anomaly The Face. The information was released to the general public in hopes it would generate interest in their exploratory work. It did, and then some.

News of NASA's discovery of a stone formation resembling a human face hit print media, television news and supermarket tabloids creating a tsunami of curiosity. To this day The Face remains a subject of considerable conjecture debate and rumor. Due to difficulties with orbital trajectories and weather patterns over the Cydonia region, future spacecraft studies didn't really persuade the public one way or the other. Does The Face provide hard evidence of a dead civilization on Mars?

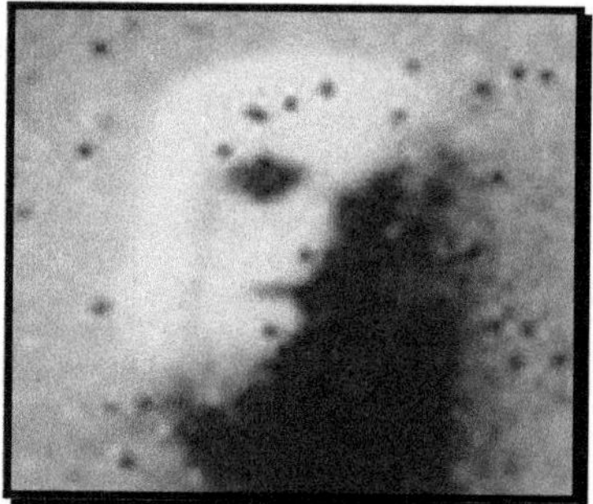

Viking 1 image courtesy of NASA

In 1977 computer engineers Vincent DiPietro and Gregory Molenaar, enhanced original NASA images of the Cydonia region and discovered two additional artifacts near The Face. One was a five-sided pyramid and the other resembled the foundational grid patterns of a small city. The five-sided pyramid was later christened the D&M pyramid in their honor.

In the early 1980's museum curator and journalist Richard Hoagland added his voice to the growing number of speculative scientists who supported the idea of artificial structures on Mars. To this day, the number of artifacts discovered on the surface of the Red Planet continues to grow as well as the number of those who believe those items provide evidence of a dead civilization.

Like many who study the NASA image, The Face intrigues me. On earth humans have been chipping away at stone and wood to create facsimiles of our own form for eons. These statues and figures have usually been created to gaze horizontally or downward at the viewer. If The Face is artificial, as many believe, why does it stare upward and outward at the sky?

Why does The Face wear what appears to be a war helmet? Does it represent a society that was hostile toward the powers of the heavens? Was The Face constructed as a symbol of a society dedicated to war - as the name of Mars has suggested throughout history? As I meditated on the meaning of The Face, the muse I'd been searching for made its presence known. This book is the result of a marriage between the actual NASA image and the whispers of something beyond its meaning – or perhaps because of it. Is it a waking dream? That is for you to decide, dear reader.

Follow me and read my tale of woe that you share not in its fate.

Chapter 1
STEALING CANDY

Cydonian history books are extremely rare, but if you're fortunate enough to find one you'll discover the Empire's colonial period really began before warp bubble propulsion became operational. The technology was still in development when their first colony ship settled into orbit around the third planet.

The world below them was huge - nearly twice the size of their home world. It's resources and primitive inhabitants were ripe fruit for the picking and Cydonia had every intention of exploiting the opportunity to obtain a valuable harvest. The Great Leader himself had said it would be as easy as stealing candy from a baby.

* * *

"Pathfinder-One is secure from undocking," Captain Abriana reported to flight control. "We're preparing for our de-orbit maneuver."

Zade and Chaudhra, her crewmates aboard the craft, programmed a high altitude approach vector into the automated equipment that would pilot them to their designated landing site. When the electronic command engaged, the machinery reversed their orbital polarity and swung them away from the colony ship that had been their home for several months. Their small craft sank into the atmosphere as anticipation rose among the team

"Do you think our mission will be as easy and profitable as we've been told," navigator Chaudhra asked.

"If you do your job, yes," Captain Abriana answered. "The primitives down there have no idea what they're sitting on or even what to do with it if they did. We do, so we have a right to take it."

"Why not mine the asteroid field instead," engineer Zade suggested.

Abriana laughed, "It's easier and cheaper to exploit local labor. It should be relatively easy to manipulate them into trading with us for the ore we want. We'll give them intoxicants and cheap baubles. In exchange they'll give us the fuel we need to build an empire among the stars. Why should we make the effort to dig it out of the ground when they can be persuaded to do the work for us?"

"Why not gather Element 92 from their oceans," Zade said. "It's my understanding there are billions of tons of it there."

"We're doing that very thing," Abriana said. "Pathfinder-Two has been assigned the task of establishing an undersea processing plant, but it'll take years for that facility to begin production. When it's completed we'll be able to siphon huge amounts of the element from the bottom of their ocean without anyone on this planet detecting the operation. By that time, our own mission will have persuaded the locals to scour all the easily mined ore from ground locations for hundreds of miles in every direction. We'll just sit here and collect it as they bring it to us. They're not very bright, you know. Certainly not as sophisticated as we are."

Indicators on his control panel soon informed navigator Chaudhra of the termination of their approach, "Captain, we've arrived at our assigned altitude over the target location."

"Begin the demonstration phase," Abriana ordered. "I'll advise flight control of our progress."

Outside their windows a bank of cumulus clouds hid the ground from view, but as they continued to descend they broke through a gap in the layer and got their first glimpse of their destination. A settlement below them was small by their standards, but sufficiently organized to support several hundred residents. Most of them appeared to be looking upward in their direction.

"They've seen us, Captain."

"Very well, let's impress them with our style."

The spacecraft performed several acrobatic turns and rolls followed by a diving descent to within a few hundred feet above the village where it hovered motionless in the air for several minutes. As intended, their aerial antics created a sensation among the observers on the ground. All attention was focused on the strange object in the sky.

"Pathfinder-One preparing for landing and first contact," Captain Abriana reported to the colony ship.

"Begin the landing procedure," she ordered her crewmates. "Let's put the ship down in that small meadow beyond the village."

Centuries later the story of the arrival of a sky chariot bearing the Sons of Heaven would become an enduring legend among the planet's inhabitants. As their culture became older and more cultivated few would accept the tale as truth – believing as they did that they alone were the highest form of civilization in the universe. On that first day, however, an attitude of awe and respect was demonstrated.

* * *

"You're not going to believe what's going on outside," Zade declared.

At the edge of the meadow a colorful procession of dancing singing locals approached the spacecraft. At the head of it a man clothed in beads feathers and animal skins twirled around and leaped into the air in an expression of primitive dance.

"They appear to be a welcoming committee," Chaudhra observed.

Abriana ordered Chaudhra to stay with the ship, "Be prepared to lift off at a moment's notice. You may have to execute our procedures for emergency evacuation. For now, consider us on yellow alert. I don't expect an attack, but if one comes you are to lift off immediately. Zade, you and I will wear side arms and communicators any time we're outside the ship."

"What do we do now," Zade asked.

"We go out and say hello."

Abriana collected a bottle of honey colored liquor, a necklace of glow-in-the-dark costume jewelry and opened the outside hatch. Everyone in the welcoming group applauded and cheered when the two Cydonians appeared in their shiny silver uniforms.

"The Leader was right," Zade whispered in amazement. "It's going to be like stealing candy from babies."

Abriana agreed, "One might hope our first contact will always be this easy."

"Always?"

"Maybe," Captain Abriana admitted. "Maybe not. We shall see."

* * *

There was no such thing as a textbook approach to first contact with an alien culture. The book hadn't been written, which is why Captain Abriana was chosen to lead the first two expeditions and publish one. In her earlier years she'd been a teacher, an educator who established a reputation for successfully reintegrating recalcitrant students back into society.

Space Service Academy recognized her skills and drafted her into service as a leader of first contact missions. She donned the uniform with reservations about yielding to military procedures. In possession of a typical attitude of academic superiority but without ever experiencing the sting of battle, she assumed the military simply didn't want to do things her way. There was a right way of doing things and a wrong way of doing things. On her second mission, Adrianna would learn the how and why of the Empire's way of doing things.

Following her retirement from Space Service, Adrianna was interviewed by investigative journalist Mimir, "How could you be so resistant to authority when you'd been so successful at persuading students in their second decade of life to accept it."

"One leads best who understands personal issues," Abriana answered. "The duty of each citizen to the state is always more important than personal opinion or advantage. One must put aside one's private bias in order to effect positive change for all."

"What if the change isn't actually good?"

"Good is defined by the state, not by individuals," Abriana reasoned. "Our Leaders have guided us from our own primitive beginnings to a destiny of empire building among the stars. We've succeeded in the past and will succeed in the future because of our tradition of collective cooperation."

"What happens when we contact an alien world that doesn't share our opinion? What happens when they don't want our guidance? Will we resort to the lash to obtain what we want from them?"

"Our presence on those worlds has always been helpful to the indigenous population even if they resist it. We've always left their culture better than we found it."

"Minus one important thing," Mimir said. "Minus their freedom to choose their own way of living. Take for example your second attempt at establishing Cydonian culture on an alien world. That didn't go as smoothly as the first mission did it?"

"No, it didn't," Captain Abriana admitted.

"Before we get into that incident can you provide my readers with a little background of your career," Mimir asked.

"Certainly. I spent my early years in the Tharsis region on the east side of Fortuna Fossae."

"My notes tell me you grew up in the city of Echus Tikvic. Is that correct?"

"Yes, but I attended university at Cimmeria in the eastern region. That's where I first gained experience with emotionally disruptive students. Speaking of students, you don't impress me as being much older than one. You're rather young for a journalist aren't you?"

"I graduated from Cimmeria University about a half year ago. This interview is my first opportunity to speak to a celebrity," Mimir conceded. "I'm told you retired from a long career about seventeen years ago. You look young for your age."

"I don't know if you're trying to appeal to my conceit or if you're giving me a compliment, but I'll take it as a tribute for the time being."

"What happened on your second mission?"

"As you know, warp bubble propulsion became operational about the time we were ready to contact a second world. Colony ships were outfitted with the new drive and pathfinder vessels were refitted to accommodate a crew of four as well as extra equipment."

"By extra equipment you really mean heavy weapons," Mimir reflected.

Captain Adriana shifted uncomfortably in her chair. She didn't like the implications of Mimir's question.

"Yes," Adriana said as she cleared her throat. "Weapons were installed on the Pathfinder ships, but they were just improved types. We had them on the first contact mission too."

"That's not what I heard," Mimir said. "You only had one type on the first mission, a sort of non-lethal stun weapon."

"That's correct," Adriana said. "The extra weaponry was an improvement as I stated."

"There were several types of heavy weapons on the new pathfinder ships, weren't there?"

"Yes. Where are you going with this line of questioning? I thought you were interested in my second encounter."

"I am, Captain. Weaponry played a big part in it. Why don't you tell me what happened from the beginning."

"Very well. Our astronomers located two planets orbiting a G-type star, like our sun, in the northern region of the Cygnus constellation. Warp driven probes identified both of them in the habitable region. Planet 1 was nearly three times the size of our home world, while planet 2 was exactly the same size as our own. Additional probe studies confirmed planet 2 was inhabited by a race of humanoids that were more developed than the first civilization we contacted."

"Space Service decided to colonize the second planet. What happened when you landed there?"

"Alpha Cygni Two is about two hundred parsecs from our home world, but the warp bubble propulsion system got us there in moments. Our colony ship popped into normal space near the planet, navigated to a stable low orbit and launched our pathfinder spacecraft toward a settlement near a large deposit of element 92."

"What's a parsec, Captain?"

"A parsec is a measure of distance. One parsec is equal to 3.26 light years."

"What was the developmental level of the civilization your team encountered?"

"Our probes led us to believe they were organized into farming communities with rudimentary knowledge of metal work and advanced construction of stone buildings."

"Were you greeted with native celebration when you landed?"

"Not at all. Repeating the successful first contact with the inhabitants of the third planet in our own solar system we disembarked from our ship carrying gifts."

"According to the historic record the locals weren't happy to see you when you landed."

"Nobody greeted us at all. None of them were visible, although our scanners revealed quite a few of them hiding in the tall trees and thick bushes. Hiding is indicative of fear. Fear is kin to violence and the situation began to be of concern to me. I ordered our navigator to stay in the ship and our weapons officer to set up a drone launcher. Zade and I lifted our packs and walked toward the main settlement."

"Zade was your engineer on the first expedition wasn't he?"

"Yes. He was a man of good character and an able technician. We'd developed a close relationship. That's why I requested his presence on the second contact mission."

"Some of the sources I've consulted suggest you and Zade had a relationship that was much closer than the usual camaraderie of commander and subordinate."

"Yes we were close – very close. It wasn't illegal and it wasn't against regulations. That particular policy hadn't been written yet, either. I won't hide the fact we were intimate."

"Emotionally intimate," Mimir stated. "Weren't you deeply attached to one another? Weren't you sexually intimate as well?"

"I believe I already answered that question, Mimir."

"Your affection for each other was a major factor in what happened next, wasn't it?"

"The matter was investigated by a board of review. It was determined that no policy was violated in the ensuing events."

"Might that be because specific policy hadn't been written yet?"

"Do you want to hear the story or not, Mimir?"

"Certainly. Please go on. You said you and Zade walked into the village."

"Yes we did. The outlying areas of the settlement were agricultural. Families lived in shabby wooden shacks. We followed a road into town that was covered with animal excretions. The conditions weren't surprising because our probes had led us to believe the animals as well as the people that tended them were as filthy and disgusting as the road we traveled. I don't know how anyone could live like that. Even the poorest of our own people don't live like that. The whole place had the most disgusting odor – like raw sewage mixed with vomit urine and stale garbage."

"What did the town look like?"

"The town was built up against the walls of a huge stone fortress. We assumed the leaders lived inside. The main gate was closed. Zade and I walked up to the gate and waited for something to happen."

"Had you encountered anyone up to that time?"

"None. The town seemed to be abandoned, but we knew people were hiding from us. They were there. They just didn't want to be seen. Zade grew edgy and I admit to a bit of anxiety myself. I called my weapons officer and ordered him to launch a drone. I also told him to prepare a second one as soon as possible."

"What happened next?"

"Nothing happened for about an hour. When our drone reported the assembly of a group of armed soldiers inside the gate I decided Zade and I should withdraw a reasonable distance from the fortress. I thought it prudent to take cover and prepare for hostile action against us."

"Your situation report described an unprovoked attack," Mimir said.

"Yes, that's correct. The gate creaked open and about fifty riders drove through at a trot. All of them brandished lances and swords in a threatening manner. A group of about a hundred infantry marched out behind them. When we realized our hope for a peaceful encounter was gone, we locked and loaded our weapons. On the walls of the fortress a large number of archers loosed arrows at us."

"Is that how you were injured?"

"Yes. I caught an arrow in my leg. Zade went down with one in his chest, but not before he managed to throw an explosive into the riders and fire a few bursts from his weapon at them. After that things got wild."

"Did you order a drone attack?"

"What do you think? Of course I did."

"Did the soldiers continue their attack?"

"Not at first. Our response had created a certain amount of confusion in their ranks. They'd never been exposed to explosives and automatic weapons fire before, but I must admit they took it well. I used the brief pause in the skirmish to try to stop my own bleeding and to examine Zade's wound, but by then he'd already died. There was blood everywhere. He never had a chance to survive. I had no idea a primitive arrow could do such damage. It must have gone straight through to his heart."

"How did that make you feel?"

"Zade and I had hoped our first contact would be a peaceful one, but it didn't work out that way. The anxiety we felt as we walked through the empty village changed to fear when we were attacked without provocation. When I realized those filthy animals had killed my Zade I decided retaliation in force was the only appropriate response."

"How many of the enemy survived your initial fire?"

"All but about twelve of the mounted troops were down. Dying animals were making a terrible amount of noise. Their fallen riders were screaming from their own injuries. A few of the infantry had suffered injury, but most of their formation was intact. They reorganized themselves remarkably well and approached me slowly under the leadership of the remaining cavalry. I must admit they were very well disciplined under the circumstances."

"Is that when you decided to use the drone as a weapon?"

"Yes. I ordered a drone attack on the remainder of the troops advancing against me. The bombing was instantaneous. Fire erupted everywhere. Smoke filled the air. One mounted soldier survived - leading ten men on foot through the smoke and haze and fire and blood.

I must admit to a moment of admiration for their valor under fire. Despite the danger and unusual circumstances I thought they conducted themselves admirably. If such a thing can be said of one's enemy I can say the sight of their determined march through death was magnificent.

They advanced on my position as the battle continued. I'd been under cover, but when I saw the result of the drone attack I stepped out of hiding and fired on the survivors with my automatic weapon. None of them walked away."

"What about the archers on the fortress wall? Didn't they attack you?"

"I think they were too disoriented by the explosions. They were certainly blinded by the smoke we brought to bear upon the battlefield below them. None of them fired at me. I used the opportunity to slip through the smoke into the surrounding woods for cover, making my way back to the spacecraft without further incident."

"Your last order on Alpha Cygni Two is regarded by some as controversial," Mimir said. "Why did you decide on such a violent response?"

"You've never been in battle have you," Abriana asked. "Have you ever been in love?"

"No to both questions," Mimir admitted. "Are you saying love and anger played a part in your decision?"

"It played all the part," Abriana said. "I make no apology for that either. When I returned to the landing zone I ordered my weapons officer to arm the second drone with a tactical nuclear weapon and to target the fortress. It was my intention to destroy it along with any of the hostiles inside. They felt safe behind their stone walls and I wanted to remove that safety from them."

"How long did it take you to get back to the pathfinder ship?"

"It took most of the afternoon. My wound made it difficult to walk despite the painkillers in my medical kit. I needed medical attention and we lifted off to the colony ship following the launch of the second drone."

"Is that how you lost your leg?"

"It is," Adriana said. "My wound was too extensive. They had to amputate my leg. As a consequence I was grounded from space flight and promoted to a supervisory post."

* * *

An environment of higher learning can promote personal philosophy, but true changes in one's character are most often forged in the furnace of pain and loss. In the same way, Captain Adriana's torturous journey back to the pathfinder ship permanently altered her attitude from peaceful pacification to ferocious unmerciful retribution.

Although the fortress was no more than three miles' walk from pathfinder's landing zone, the return journey would prove to be physically and mentally challenging. Travel on the road couldn't be attempted because Adriana feared an encounter with a party of native savages. Her wounds created a mental fuzziness as well as an agonizing limp. She kept to narrow paths and the cover of bushes and trees all the way back. Each mile etched another change in her character.

The first mile consumed her mind with widening the distance between herself and the battlefield as quickly as possible. She feared being followed, but when no signs of pursuit presented themselves she allowed herself to think about what had just happened. An uncomfortable lump began to make itself felt in her throat.

The memory of Zade's face frozen in the torment of death haunted her mind. Bloodstains from the wound in his chest covered his uniform as well as the ground where he lay. Days and months and years of sweet conversation and intimacy with her Zade mingled with the newer memory of battle and death. Never again would she enjoy his company. Never again would she hear his gentle voice or see his smiling face. The lump in her throat grew larger.

Venomous hatred of the beastly alien animals that had killed Zade welled up in her heart. Her own face assumed an affectation of deep anger and resentment. Less than half the distance to the landing zone remained when she tripped on a tree root and fell. Part of the arrow's shaft, still embedded in her leg, snapped off when she hit the ground. Spasms of excruciating pain forced an involuntary scream. The lump in her throat burst out of her eyes in a torrent of tears.

Adriana lay in the dirt struggling to get her pain under control – weeping uncontrollably under the weight of what had happened. She screamed from her own pain and she cried for Zade's death. Long deep wracking sobs issued from the core of her soul. She howled from loss and pain. She wailed from anger.

Dirty and covered with blood, Adriana's tears eventually ebbed away – completing the poignant transition begun on the battlefield. When she at last crossed her emotional point of no return she realized the degree of danger she was still exposed to and hoped no local savage had heard her sounds. She resolved to kill any of them on sight if she was discovered – adult or child, it made no difference.

Revenge, newly born in her heart, forced the Captain to her feet. She found a fallen tree branch to use as a crutch and resumed her arduous final steps to the landing zone. What would the natives do when they found Zade's body? All that was left of him would be in their hands. She hated them for it. Every painful step of the last mile cemented brutal hatred and retaliation in her heart. Never again would she cry. Never again would she consider a peaceful encounter as a necessary part of Empire building. Cooperate or die became her new motto.

Knowing the enemy would soon gather enough courage to come out of their fortress, Adriana redoubled her efforts to reach the landing zone. Raw abject hatred drove her forward. She determined to destroy the fortress and everyone in it before the sun set that day. Her pain increased in intensity, but served to drive her on. Kill them, she told herself, kill them all.

Her weapons officer and navigator came running to her aid when they saw her struggling out of the forest. Alarmed at her wounds they helped her into their spacecraft, but not before she gave her last order.

* * *

"The After-Action report submitted by your weapons officer suggested between eight hundred and one thousand people died the day of your first contact. Is that an accurate number," asked Mimir.

Adriana nodded, "the Review Board's estimate of the loss of life included the armed attack against us as well as the tactical nuclear bombing of the fortress. Our skirmish as well as the bombing resulted in the immediate death of approximately four to five hundred savages. Radioactive fallout caused another four to five hundred deaths in the weeks and months that followed."

"Was it worth that terrible loss of life?"

Adriana believed it was justified, "When other indigenous communities learned how easily we could defeat them they capitulated. They weren't as stupid as they looked. They'd learned the hard way how superior we were and accepted it. Some communities sent emissaries from distant regions to beg for peace before they themselves were destroyed. Others hid in remote locations and chewed on their humiliation."

"It's on the record Cydonia accepted the situation," Mimir said.

"Certainly. The entire planet was effectively pacified by that one incident. We were able to mine Element 92 for a very long time without any further disturbance."

"Might it be accurate to say your encounter at Alpha Cygni Two wasn't as easy as taking candy from a baby?"

"Sometimes it's necessary to kill the baby before you take the candy," Adriana said.

This time it was Mimir who became visibly uncomfortable with the conversation. He decided to end the interview with a final question.

"First contacts didn't go so easily on planets with more highly developed civilizations did they," Mimir asked.

"Those would be different stories," Captain Adriana said. "You need to remember we needed the element above all other considerations. Our methods were justified by the results."

Chapter 2
COUNCIL of the DAMNED

Once Cydonia's period of interstellar colonization began it literally took off like a rocket. Profit beyond the dreams of avarice poured into Cydonian pockets, but also created unforeseen problems. Vassal worlds under the heel of Cydonian authority expanded in number so rapidly the limited number of fleet spacecraft struggled to support it. Communication bogged down between the Cydonian home world, the fleet and administrators of colonized worlds. Corruption infiltrated the process and diminished both product and profit. In response to this crisis, The Leader acted upon a universal political principle, which suggests any calamity in government can be resolved by expanding the bureaucracy.

Two new government departments established by the Leader became controversial almost as soon as they were formed. Older established bureaucrats saw it as a threat to their position, but younger rising stars in government service welcomed the new opportunities. A General Council was assembled for the purpose of debating these issues and to establish policy for future expansion of the Cydonian Star Empire. Delegates from every province on the home world as well as colonial governors were invited to attend.

One uninvited guest, whose words were not appreciated, took advantage of moments of distraction and managed to whisper his message in the ears of attending delegates and governors.

* * *

A transport craft materialized in normal space above the Hellas Sea on Cydonia. Viewed from the ground it appeared as a bright light high in the sky drifting slowly toward the old Hesperia spaceport in the shadow of Mt. Tyrrhenus. Upon arrival its passengers were directed toward the main concourse and baggage claim area. Electric signs greeted them in their native language.

WELCOME TO THE CYDONIAN HOME WORLD.
OUR HOSPITALITY IS A COURTESY, NOT A PRIVILEDGE.
OBEY ALL LOCAL LAWS AND ORDINANCES.
VIOLATORS WILL BE PROSECUTED.
ENJOY YOUR TIME WITH US.

Three travelers walked together along the concourse following signs directing them to baggage claim and ground transport. Delicious aromas of baked food wafted through the air encouraging their appetites. Pungent floral fragrances augmented advertisements encouraging tourists to visit the garden world of the universe. The cacophony of arriving and departing travelers added to the mystique and exotic stories they'd heard at home. For each of them, it was their first exposure to a truly cosmopolitan society.

A strangely dressed man approached the three travelers as they navigated through the crowd.

"You are from Proxima Centauri Five are you not," the stranger asked.

"Yes we are," the youngest traveler responded. "How did you know?"

"Yours is the only off-world transport to have arrived this hour," the man said. "Your arrival is listed on the display panel for Arrivals and Departures."

"Yes of course," one of the older travelers said. "How can we be of help to you?"

The strange man adjusted a hood that cloaked his head and hid his face. He spoke directly to the youngest traveler, "Your destination is the Space Service training center at Tempe Terra."

"Right again," the young man admitted. "How did you know? It's not listed on any display panel."

"Air transport schedules to the Tharsis Region have changed. You should consult the Departure panels for the gate and time of your assigned flight. You must hurry or you'll miss it."

Puzzled but willing to follow the stranger's advice, the young traveler said his farewells to his older companions and hurried away.

When he disappeared around a corner the strange man addressed his next comments to the eldest of the travelers before him, "You are the Governor of Proxima Centauri Five and you are traveling to the University of Cimmeria to attend the General Council."

The Governor traded frowns and defensive eye contacts with his companion. Who was this person? Why was he dressed so strangely? What does he want from us? They didn't respond.

"You doubt my motives for approaching you," the stranger said. "You do well. You would also do well to doubt the motives of Cydonia. The future of many worlds and their people will be decided in the next few days. It does not promise to be a good one.

Those who stand with Cydonian policy will be damned – will be stripped of their resources, of their freedom to choose their own laws and of their homes. They may even be stripped of life itself. Of all these, Cydonia will suffer most when retribution returns upon the head of the Leader and the people who follow him. The world of Cydonia shall surely die.

Turn away from these proceedings. Seek ways of independence and good will for yourselves and your neighbors in space. Death walks close behind Cydonia. Beware and turn away."

Anxiety gripped the travelers as if they'd been suddenly drenched in ice water. Afraid to spend another moment in the presence of a man they believed to be mad, the Governor and his escort turned away and hurried along the concourse without exchanging another word. One of them dared to glance back at the place where they'd met the stranger, but he'd disappeared into the crowd and was not to be seen.

* * *

Colonel Zuph nervously brushed a bit of lint from his finest uniform as he waited to be ushered into an important meeting. Common citizens were seldom invited to a private audience with the Leader, which suggested he'd been selected for a special assignment. A guard opened the door in front of him and gestured for him to enter.

"Come in Colonel Zuph," the Leader said. "I've been looking forward to meeting you."

Zuph marched in stiffly and saluted. The Leader returned his salute and asked him to be seated.

"The present situation requires us to be informal for a few minutes. Would you like a hot beverage?"

"Thank you sir, I'd like that very much," Zuph said.

The Leader nodded to an assistant who returned a few minutes later with hot drinks. Zuph waited for the Leader to sip his drink before the Colonel tasted his own. Informal or not, protocol was always to be respected. The Leader always ate and drank before any of his guests.

"We've received a number of intelligence reports indicating disagreeable developments on Alpha Cygni Two," the Leader stated. "Are you familiar with the planet's history?"

"Certainly, sir. Every school child knows Alpha Cygni Two was one of the first successfully established colonies in the Empire."

"What of current events on that planet? Are you aware of the political situation?"

"I'm not sure I understand your question, sir. I've read dispatches that mention minor disputes, but otherwise the situation appears to be stable."

The subject appeared to be a matter of some irritation for the Leader who made no attempt to mask his feelings. "It isn't stable. It isn't stable at all," he said sharply. "Our military intelligence service has been able to infiltrate several civilian organizations on Alpha Cygni Two. If the information they've discovered is true, there's massive corruption at every level. There are rumors of an assassination plot against their current leadership. Governor Mahlah's death could trigger an uprising among the leaders of private estates and enterprises leading to secession from the Empire."

"Secession, sir?"

"Withdrawal from the Empire and from the Empire's authority, Colonel."

"I'm aware of the historic meaning of the word, but I confess to a bit of surprise that anyone would consider such an ill advised action in this day and age. I had no idea the situation on Alpha Cygni Two had degenerated to that level."

"It has indeed. Our space fleet is stretched almost to the breaking point and can't support military action there. Even worse, Governor Mahlah is an inept figurehead who is incapable of solving his own problems. That's why I've asked you to come here today."

"How can I be of service, sir?"

"The situation has forced me to create a new Department of Enforcement called the Cydonian State Police. Its' purpose is to establish and maintain peace on our colony worlds, to eradicate corruption and to insure the strength of the Empire.

I'm appointing you head of Cystapo operations on Alpha Cygni Two with all the authority responsibility and benefits that come with that office. You are to operate with absolute autonomy, subject only to the oversight of the Department of Finance and myself.

In order to assist you with these responsibilities, I'm promoting you to the rank of Brigadier General. You may use any method you can devise to suppress the insurrection and eliminate corruption. You will not allow secession of that world from the Empire. Corruption must end. The future of the Empire depends upon it. Do I make myself clear?"

General Zuph stood to his feet and saluted the Leader, "Sir, very clear sir."

The Leader returned Zuph's salute, "You'll receive your promotion in an official packet before the end of the day. When the Council meetings adjourn you'll accompany Governor Mahlah on his return journey to Alpha Cygni Two."

"Thank you for this opportunity to be of service, sir," Zuph said proudly.

"We'll be watching your progress very closely, General. Don't disappoint us."

* * *

Delegates Governors and their Assistants who attended the conference traveled to Cimmeria City through a subterranean pneumatic tube system. Upon arrival, each group was greeted by a government guide, who provided an orientation lecture during the final leg of their journey to the Council venues.

"Welcome to Cimmeria City," a guide said to a newly arrived group. "We'll be enjoying a brief walk to the University of Cimmeria where you'll be admitted to your respective Council locations.

Voting members from provinces of the Cydonian home world will be admitted to the Council chambers in the House of Delegates. Non-voting off-world members will be admitted to Council chambers in the House of Governors. There they'll debate issues and submit recommendations to the House of Delegates for a vote of approval or dismissal. As always, final approval rests in the hand of The Leader.

If you have questions about the University or security arrangements, please feel free to ask now."

"Why is the university underground," one person asked.

"Early in our history this planet was mercilessly pelted by meteors from the nearby asteroid field. Our First Leader devised a plan to protect us by hewing entire cities out of the living rock beneath the surface. The University of Cimmeria was established about nine hundred feet below ground and remains our oldest most esteemed center of higher learning."

"Higher learning below ground," a young Assistant joked. "That's funny."

"Not funny if you and your family are killed by an asteroid impact," the guide responded. "You've been invited here to consider serious issues, not to make jokes. If you find our arrangements disagreeable or our culture humorous, you're free to leave immediately. Do you wish to be escorted off this planet?"

"No sir," came the humbled response.

"Very well. Let's have no more frivolity. We have serious work to do. Let's get to it, shall we?"

The group moved on as the Delegate from Valles Marineris lagged behind. Not interested in lectures about local history she'd learned as a schoolchild, she was engaged in intense conversation with her Assistant. Neither of the women noticed the approach of a strangely clad man until he spoke to them.

* * *

"Rookie, get over here – front and center if you please."

"I'm here, Sergeant. Do you have an assignment for me?"

"I do. There've been a number of complaints to the police about some odd fellow who's making a pest of himself over at the university."

"Cimmeria University, Sergeant?"

"That's the one."

"What kind of complaints?"

"There's an important meeting going on over there. Influential off-world types have flown in for it and joined our own people. They're saying some strangely dressed fellow is going around whispering predictions of doom and gloom."

"Is he assaulting them or asking for money?"

"None of the complaints mention violence or unlicensed peddling. I want you to bring him here."

"Arrest him? On what charge?"

"I don't care about charges. Dream one up if you want to charge him with something. I just want that vagrant off the street until the Council meetings are over. Bring him here."

"Yes, Sergeant. I'm on my way."

* * *

Private conversations in both Council chambers were interrupted when prominent video screens switched on. An image of The Face as seen from low orbit appeared. In a lower corner of the screens a small, unfocused ball of fog coalesced into to a high-resolution reproduction of the

Leader's military crest. Martial music played in the background before during and after his address. All voices hushed in respect and expectation. What would the great man say? At exactly the appointed hour and minute he appeared on screen. No one spoke as Delegates and Governors all waited to hear The Leader's words.

"I speak today to our assembled home world Delegates and Colonial Governors," said the Leader. *"I bid you welcome to the first Council of the Cydonian Star Empire. May all your deliberations be profitable and equitable for the joint benefit of everyone who dwells in the Cydonian Co-prosperity Sphere."*

Thunderous applause and a standing ovation demonstrated universal allegiance to the Leader who paused in his speech to salute his viewers.

When the applause subsided the Leader continued, *"I salute you and your proud efforts to make a better life for us all."*

Another standing ovation and round of applause greeted the Leader's remark.

"If this keeps up we'll be standing and sitting all day without hearing a single word about new policy," an Assistant to the Governor complained. A young woman seated next to him, who'd been hired as a companion, passed her hand across his arm.

"I don't care if you don't," she said. "We can entertain each other while everyone else listens."

"Stop it," the Assistant said. "I paid for you later, not now. I'm trying to listen to what's going on."

A man dressed in odd clothing approached the couple, "What do you think you'll hear from the Leader you haven't heard already?"

The Assistant turned in his seat and saw a man in a white robe standing next to him. The robes' voluminous hood completely covered his head disguising his facial appearance, but not his voice.

"Sometimes there are new twists and turns in policy to learn about," the Assistant said. "It helps to know what's being planned. Who are you?"

"One who knows. One who warns of events to come," said the stranger.

"Warnings about what? If you're warning about being bored to death by refurbished speeches and stale slogans I have to admit I've heard them all before."

"I speak of the consequences of Cydonian ambition."

"Our Leader is encouraging the Empire to greater production and profit," the Assistant said. "He's planning expansion everywhere. It's not a secret and it comes as no surprise to anyone. Sometimes I wish a surprise or two would be revealed."

"The surprise will be in the consequences. There are some who oppose Cydonian expansion."

"Exactly who might they be? In all my travels through the universe I've never encountered a single space-faring race to equal our own. Who will oppose us? No one. Opposition might be an interesting turn of events, but there's no evidence of such a possibility."

A police officer patrolling the area spotted a man dressed in a black uniform and black helmet that covered his entire head. The uniformed man appeared to have insinuated himself into a conversation with an Assistant to one of the Council members. Aware of reports of a man making a nuisance of himself among invited guests, the officer approached cautiously.

The Assistant stood to his feet and faced the stranger directly, "Who are you sir and who do you represent?"

"Heed my warning," the robed man said. "Decisions will be made by this Council that will inevitably lead to disaster. If events proceed as planned, this entire planet will be destroyed. It will be wiped clean the way a man wipes a plate. Not one stone will be left standing upon another. Everything will be thrown down and nothing will ever live upon it again. The future of Cydonia must be peace, else war and death will return a terrible vengeance upon it."

The police officer stepped up and asked the Assistant if the uniformed man was intruding upon his privacy.

"I suppose not," the Assistant replied. "I'd just like to know who he is, that's all."

Both men turned to speak to the stranger, but he was nowhere to be found.

"Young woman," the police officer said. "Did you see where the man we were talking to went? What direction did he go when he left us?"

"What man," the woman asked. "I didn't see anybody."

On large video screens throughout Cimmeria University the Leader continued with his announcements and proposals for the future.

"It is with great pride that I announce to you today a break-through in the technology of communications. Utilizing the principles of quantum physics, we've developed a method of instantaneous communication. Distance will no longer be a limitation. It will be as easy and quick to send a message across the room as to another star system many parsecs distant. This method of communication will vastly improve the efficiency and consolidation of the Empire.

Our first presentation of this new technology will be to inform you that colony world Council members will no longer need to travel to Cydonia for Council meetings. Everyone will be able to join our sessions by way of virtual reality – enabled by instantaneous quantum communication in real time."

Once again every person in attendance at the Council meetings stood to their feet. Applause and cheers thundered across the university out into the streets and echoed off the buildings of the underground city.

A young journalist on her first assignment later wrote about the ovation. Her column suggested applause on the part of Colonial members wasn't inspired by the new technical wizardry as much as it was an expression of relief at not having to travel to the home world to listen to repetitious slogans and pontification.

Following submission of her story she was summarily dismissed from her position. Several days later, on the street in front of her residence, two women threw acid in her face.

When the cheers and clapping settled down the Leader continued, *"I also wish to announce an accelerated plan to increase the size of our space fleet. Within the coming year we intend to double the number of freight carriers and passenger vessels. We also anticipate development of two new types of military spacecraft. These new vessels will be used to defend our trade routes and to promote the Cydonian Co-prosperity Sphere to worlds with industrialized civilizations. These measures will insure the continuation and expansion of Cydonian culture and prosperity among the stars."*

This time the applause was more subdued and polite. Militarized expansion onto industrialized worlds wasn't thought to be as efficient an addition to the Co-prosperity Sphere as had been assumed by their economic planners. Uniformed warmongers never made good negotiators. In the studied opinion of many, the weaponization of space was an unacceptable enticement for expansion of the space fleet.

One Delegate was later quoted on a news program. "The risks are too great," he said. "It's possible an enterprising civilization might steal our technology, reverse engineer it and decide to take matters into their own hands. Instead of prosperity we could find ourselves engaged in interstellar war. Greed, not considered decision, is propelling us into the future."

A Colonial Governor disagreed, "Cydonian culture is exceptional. Our power is absolute. We're too big to fail. Any attempt at mutiny could be quickly and easily suppressed. I don't believe there's anything to worry about. Those who disagree with the Leader's plans for the future are defeatist cowards."

Tempers flared and debate often became over-heated and impolite. At the end of the Council meetings it was discovered that several Delegates and Governors had been admitted to healthcare centers in Cimmeria City with injuries sustained from arguments that became too enthusiastic. The Leader went on record as being pleased with the results of the Council meetings, but those records didn't reflect the opinion of many who weren't pleased at all.

* * *

A warp driven transport popped into normal space above Alpha Cygni Two's only spaceport. Appearing as a bright light in the morning sky, it had arrived exactly on schedule. The spacecraft descended slowly toward the terminal building as a group of people, who hid in shadows on the ground, prepared for its arrival.

Passengers aboard the transport began to gather their personal belongings in expectation of leaving the spacecraft. Aboard for this trip were Governor Mahlah, who was returning from the Council meetings on Cydonia as well as Brigadier General Zuph of the newly created department of the Cydonian State Police – the Cystapo. The transport settled onto the tarmac a hundred yards from the terminal building and opened its outer hatch.

"Why haven't we docked with the main building," a passenger asked.

"We've been informed by ground control of a problem with the docking mechanism," a member of the crew said. "You'll have to walk a short distance to the terminal where you can pick up your baggage and arrange for ground transport. It's a beautiful day and you can use the opportunity to stretch your limbs."

Passengers left the spacecraft in small groups. Governor Mahlah and General Zuph joined the second group. Mahlah strode out of the transport smiling and waving at news cameras and a small group of people who'd assembled to welcome his return to Alpha Cygni Two. Not wishing to be recognized, General Zuph wore civilian clothing and walked on the opposite edge of the group farthest from the clutter of service vehicles news crews and sign carrying civilians.

A sudden explosion ripped into the welcoming crowd and arriving passengers knocking all of them to the ground. Shredded metal mingled with blood and body parts flew through the air. Many who weren't immediately injured by the explosion suffered confusion and disorientation. Some of them reacted by screaming and running in all directions. Others stumbled around in the smoke and carnage not sure what had happened or where they were.

A woman, missing an arm, ran toward the terminal. Her bloody stump gushed blood that sparkled when it caught the light of the morning sun. A man with half his face missing blindly collided with a moving service vehicle and was crushed under its wheels. Several, who had been knocked to the ground, tried to crawl to safety on all fours. A young girl, who'd been impaled by a sharp bit of metal in her neck, tried to call for help. She struggled for a minute until she collapsed onto the ground where she died in a pool of her own blood. A baby with its clothing on fire screamed in the arms of its dead mother.

A group of armed people leaped out of their hiding places ran through the smoke and rushed into the spacecraft through its open hatch.

Chapter 3
REVOLT of the SHUNDITE

Little immediate concern had been expressed when the warp shuttle from Alpha Cygni Two failed to return to Cydonia on schedule. Occasional equipment malfunction, fuel handling difficulties and even severe weather patterns had been responsible for delays in the past. Before the new quantum communications equipment had been developed, it'd been impossible to exchange messages by any way other than through the hands of a courier who made the actual journey between worlds. It was an old school method of communication, but without a direct immediate comm link it was impossible to learn why the shuttle was late. When a few days passed with no news of the missing spacecraft, people in authority began to be apprehensive.

Space Service authorized the use of a small transport. As soon as it was fueled and loaded it was dispatched to Alpha Cygni Two. On board the spacecraft a team of specially trained engineers accompanied the first quantum communication unit to be installed on a colony world. A week later Phobos Station, normally tasked with monitoring message traffic, received a disturbing bulletin from the colony.

"Chief, chief can you look at this message? It's really strange."

An apple-cheeked recruit fresh out of radioman school excitedly passed a message to his Station Chief, "What do we do with this? Is this legitimate? How can we receive immediate message traffic from a planet two hundred parsecs away?"

"It's the new quantum communication circuit or QC," the Chief of Phobos Station replied. "We can expect to handle a lot more of these messages as new comm units are made available. This relay station will get very busy when we can…"

The Chief's voice faded into silence as he read the high priority message.

FROM: STATION 1 – ALPHA CYGNI TWO
CYSTAPO HEADQUARTERS 010520BGZ
BRIGADIER GENERAL ZUPH, COMMANDING

TO: CYDONIA MILITARY COMMAND
SPACE SERVICE HEADQUARTERS

ALERT BULLETIN

AN EXPLOSIVE DEVICE WAS ACTIVATED WHEN WARP TRANSPORT WT-0103 ARRIVED THIS LOCATION.

ELEVEN PASSENGERS KILLED INCLUDING GOVERNOR MAHLAH AND HIS ASSISTANT. CYSTAPO BG ZUPH WAS WOUNDED IN THE HEAD AND LEFT HAND. ZUPH IS RECOVERING FROM HIS INJURIES.

LT. GOVERNOR U'SURPAREI HAS BEEN SWORN IN AS SUCCESSOR.

LOCAL DISSIDENTS CALLED THE SHUNDITE CLAIM RESPONSIBILITY.
SHUNDITE REBELS BELIEVED TO HAVE HIJACKED SPACECRAFT WT-0103.

DESTINATION OF WT-0103 AND/OR BASE OF SHUNDITE OPERATIONS UNKNOWN.

-30-

QC TRANSCRIPTION 1 ### MLB6821

"Send this to Military Command at Space Service Headquarters," the Chief said. "Highest priority we've got. Send it NOW."

* * *

An attractive young woman sat at a sidewalk café across the street from Alpha Cygni Twos' combined Air and Space Terminal and watched the day arrive. A derelict, smelling of stale booze and sweat, staggered past her table. Throbbing noises of a delivery truck echoed off the surrounding buildings as its' driver slowly searched for a place to park his rig. Several people wandered into the café and seated themselves nearby. The sun was beginning to color the sky as a waiter placed a cup of steaming hot tea on the young woman's table.

"Be careful, it's quite hot," the waiter cautioned. "Will there be anything else?"

"In a minute. I'm waiting for someone," she said.

As she watched the terminal's employee entrance, a familiar young man left the building. She waved to get his attention. He saw her and waved back.

Disturbing rumors had reached Anna's ears, forcing her to realize it was time to leave the city. She thought the fellow she'd waved at ought to have a chance to escape as well. Others had advised her against it. He was loyal and honest, but rather dull witted when it came to complicated situations.

The young man crossed the street approached her table and wished her a good morning.

"I haven't seen you in a few days," B'anah said. "How are things going?"

"Not well. Audiences at our shows have been rather sparse the last few nights. The band is hurting for money. Our gig ended last night and we're going to break up for a while."

"I'm still working in spite of the bombing," he said. "I'm glad to have work, but some strange things have happened. I lost a whole night's work when they wouldn't let me into the building, so I snuck around the outside to see what was going on."

"What strange things?"

"They changed my hours after the bombing. Made me work the night shift."

"I know that, B'anah. You told me a week ago."

"Yes I did. Anyway I'm still working in baggage handling, but employees all over the terminal are being called out for little interviews. Nobody will talk about it. It's making me nervous."

"I've heard some rumors too," Anna said as she waved for a waiter to take her order. "That's why I wanted to talk to you this morning."

Across the street in a dilapidated building, two men hid in the shadows behind a second floor window studying the café rendezvous on the street below.

"What's that big case she dragged in with her," one asked.

"It's a stringed instrument – a large musical instrument. She's a member of a small band that entertained a nightclub a few blocks from here. Last night was their final appearance. Her group will move on today. We're supposed to pick her up when she finishes eating."

Two other men arrived in front of the terminal building.

"What did you see when you peeked around the corner of the building," Anna asked.

"An unscheduled spacecraft arrived from Cydonia and a team of uniformed men unloaded several unusual crates from it. Spaceport security locked the whole place down pretty tight. Local police wouldn't allow passengers in or out for a while. I'm also having problems getting my pay check."

An alarm went off in the back of Anna's mind. She glanced at the terminal building, "What problems?"

"They said my pay has been delayed, but that I could come in and pick it up in a half-hour. I wonder if I'm in trouble because I didn't work that one night. Do you think it means something?"

"Everything means something," Anna said as the waiter placed a breakfast sandwich in front of her. Two men malingering outside the terminal's employee entrance aroused her interest.

"Something for you sir," the waiter asked.

"Yes. Give me the breakfast special. I just got off work and I'm really hungry."

"I've been hearing rumors I need to pass on to you," Anna said quietly. "A man who was hurt in the bombing was a high ranking person of some kind."

"It wasn't in the news."

"Of course not, B'anah. The government controls the news. They only tell us what they want us to hear. They didn't want anybody to know about the man who came from Cydonia with the governor."

"The governor was killed by the bomb," B'anah said.

"I know that, B'anah. Everybody knows that. Everybody doesn't know about the other man. He wasn't killed."

"Oh. I'm glad to hear that. Who is he?"

This conversation is doing nothing to calm my nerves, Anna told herself.

"He's an officer of the Cystapo," Anna said. "It's rumored he's been assigned the task of arresting anybody involved with the rebellion."

"What's the Cystapo?"

"Secret police, B'anah. Don't you understand that a lot of innocent people are going to be arrested and imprisoned because of that man?"

"I just handle the baggage. I don't know any secrets."

"You said someone was interrogating people you work with at the terminal. You said you were nervous about it. The Cystapo might be the ones conducting those interviews."

"Do you think they'd get me fired?"

Anna lost her appetite. Caution spoke more loudly than her empty stomach and she suddenly felt the need to get away from the café as quickly as possible.

"Listen B'anah, I'm going back to the farm to visit my family."

She stood to her feet and gathered her things, "If you need to reach me, call them. My phone will be disconnected until I get enough money to activate the line again."

"What about your band? Will you get another job with the band?"

Distracted by other thoughts, she didn't answer right away. She risked another glance at the terminal building. The two men were still there, joined now by a third person.

"The band," she asked. "The band? That's right, the band – we'll get another gig. Soon, I hope."

"I hope so," B'anah said. "I hope you come back to the city real soon."

"Listen," she said. "Maybe you should take some time off and visit your folks too. I know they'd like to see you. Forget your pay. Come home with me now, B'anah."

"Oh I can't," he said. "I haven't been working long enough to get paid time off."

"Tell them you're sick or something."

"I'm lonely for my folks and the farm," B'anah said. "But I need the money. I hope you understand."

"I do," Anna said. "I really do. That's why I'm going home. I may take a few side trips to visit relatives too. I haven't seen any of them in a long time. If you call my folks and don't hear from me right away just be patient."

B'anah paid for both orders and they exchanged a long good-bye. As Anna walked down the street toward a public transportation center, the driver of the delivery truck started its engine and began to move slowly in her direction. The derelict that had passed her table came out of an alley and followed her. The two men who'd been watching from the old building descended to the street and walked briskly in the same direction.

A vehicle pulled up in front of the terminal and the three men who'd been waiting there followed B'anah through the employee entrance.

* * *

"What am I doing here," B'anah protested angrily. "Why am I fastened to this chair? Am I under arrest?"

Three men faced him in a darkened room. One of them jabbed a hypodermic needle into his arm.

"What's that for," B'anah yelled. "Why am I here?"

"What's your name," one of the men asked.

B'anah felt his hands and feet grow strangely warm and numb.

"What's happening to me? What are you doing to me," he demanded.

Making demands and asking heated questions gave him a terrible headache – like nails driving through his skull. He began to get the idea it was wrong to resist the men around him. It hurt to be angry. It felt good to cooperate.

The question was repeated, "What's your name?"

"Name. My name is B'anah," he said as his mind became fuzzy. It felt good to admit to the truth of who he was. He didn't want to resist any more questions. There was no sensation from his knees to his feet and from his elbows to his hands. He felt good and he didn't want to complain about it any more.

"Who's the girl you met at the café? How do you know her?"

B'anah was becoming drowsy, "Anna… from home. From the farm next door."

"What did you tell her about the warp shuttle? Did you tell her who would be on board?"

"Yes. She asked about...passengers…arrival times...I told."

"Why did she want to know those things?"

"I don't know. We just talk."

B'anah's eyesight was blurry. It was difficult to keep his eyes open. He couldn't feel his arms below his shoulders or his legs below his waist. He felt very sleepy. One of the strange men unfastened his bonds from the chair. B'anah's arms fell limp at his sides. The chair was so comfortable he didn't want to escape it.

"How do you feel about Cydonian rule of this planet? Do you know people who are opposed to it?"

"Don't think about … Cydonia. Only work and sleep. No friends here."

"How about at home on the farm? How do your friends feel about Cydonia?"

"Friends gone to city work. Parents too old to care."

"What about Anna? Are her friends loyal?"

Sensation had completely disappeared below B'anah's neck, but he had to answer the question. He felt a strong compulsion to talk, "Which friends?"

"Anna's friends. How do they feel about Cydonian authority?"

"Farm friends busy – farming.   Music friends I don't know."

"How does she feel about Cydonian authority?"

It was hard to even talk now, "No … talk Cydonia. Only talk… shuttle schedule … passengers..."

B'anah's chin flopped down onto his chest. His breathing became labored. He lost consciousness.

"He's close to death sir, shall I revive him with the antidote?"

"No," came the answer. "Let him die. I don't want him to alert anyone about our interest in this matter. When he dies dispose of his body at the fertilizer plant with the other refuse of his animal race."

"What if they ask questions?"

"We're Cystapo. We ask questions. We don't answer them."

* * *

An inner door to the office of the Cystapo commander snapped open followed by a deep throaty voice from within inviting agent Do'ega to enter. The fledgling agent had heard rumors about the general, but his first encounter with the man in no way calmed any of his anxieties. Mid-morning's crisp light streamed through the office windows into his eyes, temporarily blinding his first steps into the inner chamber.

Do'ega squinted and stepped through the beam of bright light. Beyond the light was revealed in potent detail the entire extent of the injuries sustained by the General on the day of his arrival. Zuph looked every bit as gruesome as the office he commanded.

The bomb's blast had entirely torn away Zuph's left ear. Its' former location had been surgically obscured with the ruddy pink skin of a graft still in the process of healing. His left eye had been damaged beyond remedy. Doctors had suggested replacing the eye with a cosmetic implant, but he'd refused. Instead, he chose to wear a black eye patch, which projected an affectation of subdued hostility.

When the bomb exploded small bits of super heated metal plowed into his face ripping through some of it and burning the rest. Partial healing developed ugly scars bridged by the frozen remnants of melted flesh that had poured over the torn skin like liquid plastic. Zuph had chosen to bare his face to those he met rather than cover it or have it surgically repaired. The changes to his face caused by his injuries presented an appearance of hideous potent evil. General Zuph wore it as a badge of perverse honor.

"Good morning agent Do'ega," Zuph said. "I understand you have new information about the Shundite rebels. Please be seated."

"Thank you, general," Do'ega answered nervously. "We've made some significant progress, but there's more to learn."

"Start with what you know," Zuph said.

"During Governor Mahlah's administration Shundite rebels disrupted mining, fuel refinement and transportation operations to a significant degree. Rebel actions were successful because they'd been well coordinated. Their coordination required communication between groups in separate cities as well as individuals within the cities.

Mahlah's efforts to learn the identity of individuals in those groups as well as their method of communication were painfully ineffective. All attempts to intercept or detect electronic communications between the Shundite groups failed. I'm pleased to report we've discovered how it was done."

"You have my attention agent Do'ega. Please continue."

"The assassination of Governor Mahlah proved to be a windfall event because it focused our investigation upon employees of the air and space terminal. One of them had access to the passenger lists as well as regular contact with a person we'd already suspected as being a Shundite sympathizer. Under interrogation he admitted he'd passed passenger information and the warp transport arrival time to that person – a woman he called Anna.

Prior to this confirmation we'd placed Anna under continuous surveillance. I searched her personal effects myself. I did so without approval or application for legal search and I hope this doesn't reflect negatively upon this department."

"You're a Cystapo agent, Do'ega. You don't need anyone's permission," Zuph added. "Please continue with your report."

"Certainly sir, thank you sir. We searched her leased living spaces and didn't find anything. They were clean, as though an official search was expected. I even examined her musical instrument. When I found nothing unusual about the instrument I decided to install a tracking device inside one of the f-holes."

"F-holes, Do'ega? What are f-holes?"

"Anna accompanies a musical group and plays a large stringed instrument. The surface of the instrument has large decorative holes beside the strings so as to allow vibrations of sound from within to escape. These decorative openings are called f-holes. I have small hands and could reach inside the f-holes to install a small tracking device. When I did, I discovered pieces of paper attached to the inside of the instrument. The paper had unencrypted writing about the assassination as well as information about future rebel activity. Paper would not normally be detected by standard security devices at any check-points Anna passed through."

"You said the writing wasn't encrypted?"

"That's correct, general. Not encrypted or encoded at all."

"Why not?"

"I suppose it's because of the nature of the Shundite movement. The word Shundite suggests one who is multi-lingual and multi-traditional. Various groups are linked to one another in opposition to the Empire via the rebellion. Each of these groups has an individual language and social tradition, but work together to support the whole, hence the term Shundite. The paper notes Anna is passing around aren't encrypted because it would be more difficult for the information to be understood if it had been encrypted in some way."

"What are you planning to do with this discovery," Zuph asked.

"We've already identified all the principle members of the groups and intend to begin arrests and punitive action very soon. Interrogation of these persons will give us the names of minor members. It shouldn't take more than a few weeks to put an end to the rebellion here on Alpha Cygni Two."

A thin painful smile appeared on Zuph's disfigured face, "Excellent work agent Do'ega. At the beginning of this meeting you said there was more to learn. What more is there to learn?"

"The first part is easy, general. We've learned former Lt. Governor, now Governor U'Surparei is implicated in some of the rebel activities. He's motivated by personal aggrandizement rather than an attempt to usurp Cydonian authority, but his involvement is certain. Although we don't believe he was directly involved in the bombing, he's benefited from it nonetheless. His advanced position as governor will allow him much influence with the rebels as well as financial windfalls. What should we do with this information, sir?"

Zuph didn't hesitate, "Arrest him. Take him out to the street in front of the governor's residence and execute him publicly. Let his body rot where it falls. Find some mental defective to take his place and inform my office."

"Yes sir."

"What's the last matter, agent Do'ega? You've been avoiding the subject. Let's have it."

"We don't know where the Shundite rebels took the warp shuttle, sir. The situation is complicated and we have only a basic idea as to how to proceed with our investigation."

"What's complicated about it?"

"It's easy to hijack a warp shuttle. The rebels demonstrated what was once considered an implausible act is a very real possibility. A more important question is to ask where it went and how the rebels learned of a destination."

"Cydonia is the only spacefaring race in the universe we're aware of," Zuph said. "One of the subjects of debate at the recent Council meetings was whether or not we should colonize industrial worlds. One side argued they'd make good partners, but the other side argued it would be too easy for them to capture one of our vessels and reverse engineer it to learn our secrets. Are you suggesting one of those worlds had something to do with it?"

Do'ega shrugged his shoulders, "We doubt any direct involvement, sir."

"What's that supposed to mean? Stop being coy with your assumptions, agent."

"First of all there's no known world that would be able to adapt our technology. I'm told we've investigated a few candidates for colonization and are preparing for first contact, but none of them are advanced enough to understand the basic principles of space travel.

Secondly, we've investigated astronomers and astrophysicists on Alpha Cygni Two in the hope we could glean some information about possible rebel destinations for the warp shuttle, but all those people are too focused on their work to be interested in the political situation. They're all clean.

We're convinced the rebels learned enough about a suitable destination to hijack a shuttle and navigate across the vastness of space to get there. We don't know where this knowledge may have originated."

"Those are very dangerous lines of inquiry, agent Do'ega. You must pursue them as far as they take you. The future of the Empire may depend upon it. Consider it top priority. We can't allow potential enemies to lurk among the stars. Use any methods and resources you need to discover it."

"I have one last question General."

"Name it."

"We have arrested the girl Anna. How do you want us to dispose of her - case?"

"Bring her to me," Zuph said. "I have a few questions of my own to ask."

* * *

The Cystapo reign of terror began on Alpha Cygni Two.

Core leaders of the Shundite rebellion in every city were arrested and publicly executed without hearing trial or appeal. Bruised and bleeding from hours of abuse, with their bodies clad only in ragged strips of clothing, they were hung from lampposts and advertising signs until they died. They'd remain in their position of elevated government scorn until the carrion birds had feasted on their fetid flesh and their bleached bones had fallen to the ground. Torture was common and frequent. Neighbor betrayed neighbor as each report of insurrection and sedition resulted in an arrest or the threat of imprisonment.

Businesses and private industries across the planet were required to provide funding for the establishment of forced labor camps. These same businesses and industries benefitted from the slave labor that served them. Profits rolled in. Mining and refinement of the element as well as minerals and metals needed to produce spacecraft and all the infrastructure of the Empire reached unprecedented levels. Tyranny became exceptionally good for business.

Anyone who was suspected of being sympathetic to the Shundite rebellion was arrested – usually in the middle of the night. Cystapo agents seized the private assets of those who were detained. Their homes were demolished and their children taken into custody. Minors between the ages of ten and twenty were enrolled in martial training facilities where they could either accept militarism as a personal philosophy or graduate to a forced labor camp for the rest of their natural lives. Children under the age of ten were confiscated and transferred to retraining facilities on Cydonia. On the home world, they'd forget their families and early homes. In time they'd become proud patriotic citizens of the Cydonian Star Empire.

Nearly every action taken by the Cystapo reaped the benefits they desired. All resistance to Cydonian authority collapsed. No longer were the efficient and profitable engines of the Empire impeded. For the most part, Brigadier General Zuph was satisfied with the results of his program to bring Alpha Cygni Two under the heel of the Cydonian Empire – mostly, but not completely. There remained a final interview with a rebel named Anna as well as a nagging mystery.

The mystery lingered as to where the hijacked warp shuttle had been taken and how the Shundite rebels had determined its destination. The application of torture and persecution had resulted in the elimination of rebel activity, but no real answers to the mystery. Cystapo inquisitors were told only what their victims thought they wanted to hear. Nothing of substance was learned. Nobody knew anything, apparently. Zuph hoped that when agent Do'ega hauled Anna into his office he'd learn something. Everything had gone as planned – almost everything.

* * *

Anna was dragged into General Zuph's office in chains. The general expected her first impression of him to be one of shock and disgust, but when she didn't react to his appearance he simply offered her a seat.

"I prefer to stand, General."

Zuph nodded to the guard who'd brought her in. The guard produced a baton and struck her in the knee with it. Anna screamed and fell to the floor.

"When I extend a trifle of hospitality I expect it to be accepted. Sit in the chair or grovel on the floor like an animal. It's up to you, rebel."

Anna stood slowly to her feet, but refused to sit in the chair. After another nod from the general she was struck down again.

"We can do this all day," Zuph said. "I want to ask you a few questions. Your treatment hereafter will depend upon your answers and your attitude. Sit in the chair or bleed on the floor. It's up to you."

Zuph signaled to the guard who exchanged his baton for a spiked whip. The guard prepared to strike Anna with it.

"What do you want to know," Anna said painfully.

"I understand you are acquainted with a young man by the name of B'anah, formerly employed as a baggage handler at the Air and Space Terminal."

Anna replied that she knew a young man by that name.

"You should be informed that he is presently contributing to the agricultural economy of Alpha Cygni Two," General Zuph said.

"He's working on a farm?"

"In a manner of speaking, yes. Following his death during interrogation his body was delivered to a local fertilizer plant where it was processed into a form which now serves the Empire in a more useful capacity."

Anna had expected news of that nature, but actually hearing it from the lips of a hideous beast was more than her weakened condition would allow. She wept.

"Tears for a traitor," Zuph observed. "How touching. I wonder how many tears you shed for those who died in the bombing. Can you weep for my injuries as well?"

Anna spit on the floor where she lay.

General Zuph nodded to the guard who laid a heavy stroke on her back. Razor sharp spikes embedded in the whip tore through Anna's clothing and skin. Anna screamed. Blood began to stain her clothing. Large drops of it fell to the floor forming small red pools.

"I'm just a messenger," she said. "That's all I've ever been. I haven't damaged any government property or hurt anyone. I haven't made speeches and I haven't recruited any members. I just passed messages, that's all."

"Those messages were crucial to the operation of the rebel groups on this planet. Some of those messages contained valuable information. You read those messages and you remember what they said."

"I didn't read them. All I did was pass them along."

"Certainly you discussed the contents of those messages from time to time. I'm interested in one particular subject – the hijacking of the warp shuttle."

"I don't know anything about that," Anna said.

Zuph nodded and the guard struck Anna again. Shreds of flesh were torn away from her back and flew into the air when the guard withdrew his whip. Anna screamed and collapsed fully upon the floor.

"One more of those and you'll need a doctor," Zuph said.

"You're the one that needs a doctor," Anna replied.

"You're full of spit and vinegar, aren't you," Zuph said. "That'd be commendable if you were performing for a rebel audience, but there are none here. Your venom is wasted in this office.

I'm here to promote Cydonian civilization and its laws. You're here because you're trying to destroy it. Where did your rebel friends take the warp shuttle?"

"I don't know anything about the warp shuttle," Anna repeated. "I don't believe you know anything about civilization either. What we've got on Alpha Cygni Two isn't one we've chosen for ourselves. It's better to be uncivilized than to live in the one you've forced upon us."

"Your pitiful attempt to seize power has failed," Zuph pointed out. "We've destroyed the entire Shundite organization – literally burned it down and buried it in servitude. Whether you like it or not you're subject to Cydonian law."

"You haven't destroyed everything," Anna said. "People die. Ideas live on. A bit of life and hope always remains. Can Cydonia always win? No. A remnant will linger in the shadows. Others will be born later who'll dream again the dream of our own kind of civilization. Cydonia will be challenged one day and Cydonia will be chased all the way back to its home world. Cydonia will suffer destruction it has earned for itself."

"You are full of angry words," Zuph said. "But civilization rests in the hands of Cydonia and our hands are strong."

"What civilization and until when," Anna said.

"I'll ask you for the last time," Zuph demanded. "Where was our shuttle taken?"

"I'll tell you all I've learned from the others," Anna admitted. "I can tell you what we've told each other. They say it's better to know where to go and not know how to get there than to know how to go and not know where."

"That tells me something," Zuph said. "The stolen warp shuttle was the way to get there. How did your rebel friends learn where to go? Tell me so we can learn too. Stop playing at words."

Anna coughed up blood, "Words are all I have now, general. The game is over."

Zuph's patience ended abruptly, "Take her out and hang her. We'll learn from others what we need to know."

As they led Anna out she gathered all her remaining strength and cried aloud, "A rebel can only lose her life, but a general can lose his whole civilization."

Chapter 4
PHOBOS and BEYOND

"You look so handsome in your new uniform, " Adrienne said as she wrapped her arms around Rauf's neck. She kissed him as tears poured out of her eyes like a river, "I've missed you so much. You've been away too long."

Rauf held her close and didn't say anything. Duty on Phobos Station had been too cold too impersonal and too far from home for too long. Her scent filled his head and he realized he'd forgotten about too many good things. Holding her in his arms with her lips on his was one of them.

Swarms of people swirled around them in the terminal concourse, but the young couple saw only each other. A few travelers noticed them and smiled.

"Almost two years," Rauf said. "It seemed to last forever, but it's only a moment now."

"Are you hungry," Adrienne asked. "You look so thin."

"Our food is adequate, but tasteless. Hardly worth the effort of eating."

"I packed a lunch," she said. "There's a pretty little park outside where we can sit and eat."

They collected Rauf's kit at baggage claim and with Adrienne's guidance found a table in the park. She offered him something she'd made. It was incredible. The sensations it's tastes created in his mouth were beyond belief.

"What did you put in this stuff," he declared. "This is wonderful."

Before he knew it he'd eaten everything she'd packed.

She laughed, "I've never seen anybody so hungry."

He wiped his mouth and apologized, "You didn't eat anything, Adrienne. I'm sorry I was so selfish."

Adrienne laughed and cried all at the same time, "I forgive you."

He used a clean napkin to gently pat away the wetness on her face.

"Is your food really that bad," she asked.

"Let me put it this way," he said. "Mashed potatoes aren't supposed to make noise when you eat it."

They sat together without a word. There'd be time to catch up on little things later. Hands held hands not desiring anything but reassurance of the others' presence. Adrienne ran her fingers over the soft fabric of Rauf's uniform.

"This isn't just a new uniform," she realized. "This is entirely different."

He brushed a crumb off his tunic, "Yes, it's the uniform of an officer - junior grade."

"When did this happen?"

"Just before I shuttled down from Phobos. It's a surprise."

She paused before asking if he'd reenlisted to get the promotion. He was proud of his new rank. She could see it in his face. She could see it in the way he carried himself.

"I'm going to be here for a little while," he said. "I've been assigned additional training before…"

She suddenly realized what the promotion meant, "Before they send you out again."

"Yes. On the newest and largest warp ship ever built, the Battlecruiser Olympus Mons."

Adrienne wept.

"What's wrong? Why are you crying?"

"You'll leave soon and I won't see you again - ever. You don't understand do you?"

"Understand what? There'll be a deployment, but nobody has said how long it will be. A career in Space Service as an officer is an extremely rare opportunity."

"I love you Rauf. Every hour you're away from home is an agony for me. I thought you felt the same way. When you left us you said your contract was only for two years. You said you'd come home again after your little adventure."

"I learned a lot about myself during those two years. I learned about duty to the Leader and about personal opportunities among the stars. I learned I wanted to be part of the Space Service."

"You mean they got into your mind and changed it."

"I was in love with the stars long before I left Cydonia. You've known that since we were young. Besides, I've sworn an oath as an officer."

"What about the promises we made to each other? Aren't they worth something?"

Rauf lost his tongue and didn't know how to answer. Adrienne collapsed in grief as though she was mourning the loss of someone who'd died. Rauf stood to his feet and walked a short distance away. Small groups of travelers shuffled in and out of the terminal building next to the park. One of them, a strangely dressed fellow, seemed to be walking toward the park.

Rauf tried to compose his thoughts, but new emotions clouded his mind. His promotion had come at an unexpectedly high cost. For the first time, serious doubts about his decision to make the Space Service a career occurred to him. He loved Adrienne dearly and he hadn't meant to cause her pain. What could he do?

The stranger approached and spoke directly, "Hello Rauf. Welcome home."

"Thanks, but I don't believe I know you."

"Correct sir. You don't know me," the stranger replied.

"If we haven't met then how do you know my name? Are you an agent of the Cystapo? Are you here to investigate my activity?"

"I'm not part of your government. One might say I work independently."

"Why are you here? What do you want from me?"

"I'm not here to get something from you. I'm here to give something to you."

"Oh, you're a riddler – one of those people who likes to ask questions without answers."

"Not unlike you," the stranger replied. "You're asking yourself questions without answers."

Rauf was taken aback. How did the stranger know what he'd been thinking? He decided not to say anything at all.

"Your silence speaks loudly," the stranger continued. "You've just realized you're standing before two divergent paths in your life and can only walk one of them. Your decision today will affect the rest of your life. Shall you enjoy the love of a good woman and the comfort of a family or will you attempt to add your name to those who've conquered the stars?"

"Why can't I have both," Rauf asked.

"Because space is cold and lonely. You already know this. Space is also very dangerous. You've heard stories from veterans, but you haven't experienced any of it personally. You may be dressed in an officer's uniform, but you are as green as grass among those who risk their lives in the great gulf between worlds. You know this to be true, but in your youthful pride you haven't seriously considered the risk."

"What risk?"

"Is Space Service worth risking your life? Those who rule whole worlds are not inspired by altruistic motives. The Cydonian Star Empire has begun to descend into a bottomless pit of debauchery and self-aggrandizement that cannot end except in annihilation."

Rauf was shocked at the language the stranger used to describe his government, "you are speaking sedition, sir."

"I speak truth," the stranger said. "You will learn much more in days to come no matter which path you choose to take. How will you find comfort then? Will you find it in the arms of your family or will you be forced to bear it alone without hope of solace?"

"I don't understand," Rauf said.

"The uniform you now wear will be the only comfort that will cloth you in space," the stranger said. "The young woman who loves you can give you much more. Look upon her."

Rauf turned his head to look at Adrienne. She was holding her head in her hands as though she'd lost all that she'd hoped for in life.

"The future will not go well for the Empire. This world will end ingloriously," the stranger said. "Those who invest themselves in the small precious things of life will know a bit of peace before it ends. Mark my words young man. It will end no matter which path you take today. Your reward or the lack of it will be found in the places between now and then."

Rauf turned back to speak to the stranger, but he'd vanished.

"What is this," Rauf yelled. "Where did you go?"

Adrienne heard Rauf's voice and came to meet him, "Are you all right? Who were you talking to?"

Rauf seemed to hear a whisper in the wind, "It's time to choose."

"There was a strangely dressed man here," Rauf said. "He came to me and said strange things."

"What man," Adrienne said. "I didn't see anyone."

Rauf looked around, trying to discover where the stranger had gone, "He was here. I talked to him."

Adrienne scooped Rauf's hand into hers, "Come home with me. You've been working too hard for too long. You need rest."

She led him away from the park, but Rauf kept looking over his shoulder. Where had the stranger gone? What did he mean when he spoke of global annihilation? Rauf looked at the world around him with new eyes and began to weep at the thought of loosing it. Adrienne didn't know what was going through Rauf's mind, but she held him in her arms and tried to comfort him anyway. He acted as though he'd suffered a nightmare fully awake.

In the years to come, Rauf would occasionally awaken in the middle of the night – covered in sweat, terrorized from dreams of fire and death. Adrienne would try to quiet his fear. Slowly and gradually he would relax and fall into a peaceful sleep in her arms.

The stars above their home looked down in cold unsympathetic indifference. Somewhere out there, men Rauf had once called friend and comrade risked their lives and died. The stars didn't care about them either. Neither did the Leader to whom they'd pledged their allegiance and who had sent them to their death.

* * *

The sky above Proxima Centauri 5 glittered with the reflected light of a newly formed Cydonian fleet as its warp ships emerged into normal space. Several of the orbiting vessels, including the newly commissioned Battlecruiser Olympus Mons and the heavy cruisers Hellas and Sabaea, were so large their outline could be seen from the planet's surface with the unaided eye. Others appeared as smaller points of light flying in formation with their bulkier sister ships.

Commanding officers and staff from each vessel boarded personnel shuttles and descended to the surface to attend briefings and strategy updates. At issue was the honing of different experimental strategies for adding industrialized worlds to the Empire. A mysterious closed session would address a matter that couldn't be considered even over the impenetrable channels of military QC/quantum communications.

Admiral Ittai, Commander of the Combined Colonial Fleet and Grandson of Captain Abriana who'd first colonized Alpha Cygni 2, marched onto a small platform in front of the assembled ship commanders and called the meeting to order.

"Good morning.

We're assembled here today to organize three operations culminating in the addition of industrialized worlds into the Cydonian Co-Prosperity Sphere. The result of the actions we begin here today will be evaluated and incorporated into procedures for future acquisitions. Our orders come directly from the Leader and will not be changed or rejected. They're to be executed as efficiently and speedily as possible.

Group assignments are as follows:

Heavy Cruisers Sabaea and Hellas will accompany Assault Vessel Chaos to begin a forced incursion on Epsilon Eridani 6.

Light Cruiser Chryse will travel to Beta Hydri 5 to accomplish colonization by means of covert methods.

Battlecruiser Olympus Mons will remain in orbit here as a reserve unit.

Agents of the pathfinder ships b'Eleh and Sorge will accompany me to secure quarters for a briefing on their classified duties.

If there are no questions you will break out to your respective group commands and make final plans for acquisition of your assigned worlds and their populations. Orbital departure is scheduled to commence in forty-eight hours.

You are dismissed."

Attendees of the meeting broke up into separate groups to discuss operational plans. Two junior officers from the Battlecruiser Olympus Mons, which hadn't been assigned a task, loitered at a food table prepared for the meeting. Few had sampled its delicacies, but that didn't appear to deter the young men. When most everyone had departed the meeting room they swapped rumors they'd heard and suspicions those rumors had aroused.

"Did you notice Admiral Ittai called the commanders of the pathfinder ships 'agents' instead of captains?"

"I don't think they're pathfinder ships," officer Statler said.

"Right, and I don't think their commanders are from Space Service," officer Waldorf admitted. "Why don't you believe the b'Eleh and Sorge are pathfinder ships?"

"Pathfinder ships don't normally carry extra fuel pods or unusual electronic equipment."

"How do you know these things?"

"I've been seeing a young recruit who's stationed in the Combat Information Center. We meet during the night watch and she told me some interesting things about the configuration of those two ships."

"You're supposed to be sleeping when you're off duty at night. What were you two doing alone in the dark?"

"None of your damn business, Waldorf. Listen to me, will you?"

Waldorf smiled, "Yea, ok. Have it your way. What did she tell you?"

"She saw scans of those ships and overheard talk about them in the officers' wardroom. They've been fitted out with scanning devices that can detect the faint traces of a warp bubble."

Waldorf laughed, "You mean like soap scum in a wash tub?"

"No, stupid. Keep your laughing quiet will you. We can't be heard talking about these things."

"Alright, but what are warp bubble traces?"

"When a very large aircraft flies through the air it leaves disturbed eddies behind it."

"I know. It's like a boat moving through the water creating a wake behind it."

"Exactly. The same principle applies when a warp bubble disturbs the fabric of time and space. Eddies in the continuum leave evidence of the passage of a warp ship behind. They don't last very long and they're very faint, but they're there."

"Are you saying those pathfinder ships are built to sniff out warp ships? Why?"

"That's the big question isn't it? But that's not all they're set up to do. They're carrying heavy weapons – weapons powerful enough to destroy a warp ship. Battlecruiser Olympus Mons is standing by in case they encounter something they can't handle."

"That makes sense," Waldorf admitted. "It would explain the different chain of command for those ships."

"What do you mean?"

"Admiral Ittai called their commanders agents because they're Cystapo ships. They aren't ships of the line, like all the rest – like ours."

"Why would Space Service equip two pathfinder ships with that kind of equipment and give command of them to the Cystapo?"

"That's obvious isn't it? They aren't pathfinder ships at all. They aren't going out to colonize another world. They're looking for a warp ship. When they find it they're going to blow it to bits."

Both men were silent as they gathered a bit of food and left the room. Outside they exchanged a few final words.

"What ship? Where would they go to find it? What's so important about it?"

"I don't know. Apparently it's a secret. I haven't heard anything about a mutiny or some ship gone missing, have you?"

"Not a peep. Not a word. Not even a rumor. I wonder what's going on."

"I wonder too, but I think we should keep our curiosity on low heat don't you? If the Cystapo is involved it could be unhealthy to ask questions."

"All things come to he who waits," Waldorf said. "Sooner or later new rumors will reach our ears. We'll need to swap stories when they do."

* * *

Light Cruiser Chryse emerged into normal space above Beta Hydri 5 and assumed a low orbit.

As soon as their flight plan had stabilized, Captain T'Sha issued orders via closed comm circuit to the Cartography Department, "I want a detailed scan of the surface with special attention paid to waterways and reservoirs. Have there been any changes since our last geographic survey of this planet? If so, I want our database updated immediately. You have one orbit to complete the task."

He sent his second order to the Combat Information Center and asked for observations and updates on the Beta Hydri 5's satellite network.

"We have less than three orbits to complete our tasks," he announced via the Intership comm system. "Let's get to work."

In the equipment bay, crewmembers were hard at work preparing a number of droids for entry into Beta Hydri 5's atmosphere. Contents of their warheads had been stored in specially refrigerated containers and could only be exposed to room temperature for a few hours before they lost their potency.

"Captain on deck," a crewman announced as Captain T'Sha walked into the bay. Those who weren't occupied snapped to attention.

"As you were," Captain T'Sha said. "How are preparations proceeding?"

"We're ahead of schedule Captain," an Ensign replied. "May I ask what we're going to do with these droids?"

"You're new aboard the Chryse aren't you," Captain T'Sha observed.

"Yes sir. I came aboard at Proxima Centauri 5 after graduating from officer training school. I haven't been briefed on our orders."

"Beta Hydri 5 will be a new addition to the Cydonian colonial Empire. We're preparing to motivate its' population to join us peacefully."

"They're rather well developed aren't they, sir?"

"Yes. They have rudimentary knowledge of space flight and have established a satellite network for civilian and military use. Their technology has improved dramatically over the past few decades. Unfortunately they continue to make war upon each other. As a consequence they have well developed strategic and tactical battle skills. It would be difficult to convince them to join the Empire by force of arms."

"How are we going to persuade them to join us, Captain?"

"These droids will deliver an active biological agent into their waterways and urban reservoirs. Within a few months the entire population of the planet will be infected with a deadly disease. A few months later their economy will be in ruins and their governments will be on their knees. At that point in time we'll appear above their capital cities and offer a cure in exchange for their participation in the greater Cydonian Co-Prosperity Sphere."

"It sounds too easy."

"When they agree, and we hope they will, Cystapo agents will be gradually insinuated into their society and governments. Eventually they'll be a willing patriotic colony of the Cydonian Empire."

"Will we remain here until the plague takes effect?"

"Not at all. We risk detection if we stay in orbit too long. In less than three hours we'll return to Proxima Centauri 5. After that we'll just sit back and let the kettle simmer, as it were."

"Millions will die, sir. Is that acceptable?"

"Our Leader has ordered it and that's all we need to know," Captain T'Sha said. "Besides, it'll be a peaceful death for them – much better than the violence they constantly visit upon themselves, but death nonetheless. The industrial infrastructure will remain intact allowing us to assume control with little or no resistance. It's a beautiful plan. We just quietly walk in and take what we want. The plan is elegant in its' simplicity."

* * *

Epsilon Eridani 6 was the first instance of a Cydonian invasion employing military force on a planet-wide scale. Much internal debate had preceded the action, as it was feared by some that it's cost in terms of blood and treasure would be excessive. Others, who won the argument, believed the campaign would be quick. Proponents of war believed immediate access to resources and industrial capacity was worth the risk. Previous acquisitions had required years of preparation building and indoctrination before worlds were fully productive. Persuaded to experiment with a more rapid expansion of the Empire, the Leader approved the attack.

Heavy Cruisers Sabaea and Hellas settled into orbit above Epsilon Eridani 6 and prepared to begin an aerial bombardment of several small cities. The assault vessel Chaos appeared in normal space and awaited completion of the bombardment before landing its troops. On the last night of peace before the invasion commenced, Commodore Jadzia addressed the crew and combat units of all three ships under her command.

"To the men and women of the Hellas Sabaea and Chaos I send greetings.

Our Leader has commissioned a great experiment – the first in our illustrious history. We've arrived at Epsilon Eridani 6 to take its resources and population by force so as to promote its ultimate prosperity as well as our own. The future of the Empire will depend upon our success or failure here. We've planned carefully and prepared completely for action. It will now be up to you to bring the hopes of all Cydonia to fruition.

The civilization below us is in the initial stages of industrial development. Industry and transportation are powered by steam engines. Their communication network is based on wired transmission of messages via simple dots and dashes. Military weaponry is based upon chemically propelled projectiles both large and small. In short range engagements they're quite effective. It's our intention to keep confrontation at a distance so as to take full advantage of our more efficient weaponry and reduce our own losses.

Our operations will begin with a bombardment of several small cities on different continents. In the first phase we'll deploy Enhanced Radiation Weapons or Neutron bombs as they're called in the common vernacular. Ignition of these bombs is lethal to all living tissue. On the other hand, damage to buildings, transportation and communication centers and resource sites are minimal. Neutron radiation dissipates quite rapidly and will allow our shock troops to secure the affected cities before their military can react.

The second phase of invasion will be to use the existing communication networks of Epsilon Eridani 6 to transmit an ultimatum to the capital of each nation demanding surrender. Failure to comply will result in the third phase – deployment of a thermonuclear device on a major city of each continent. It's hoped that a minimum demonstration of our ability to visit death and destruction will force a complete surrender without having to put boots on every inch of the planet.

We intend to repeat the process of demand and destruction until the inhabitants surrender or they're all dead. Either way, we win.

It's worth remembering that the role of the Cydonian armed forces has been and always will be to keep the Empire safe for our economy and open to our cultural assault of other worlds. To those ends, we will do a fair amount of killing.

We are on the eve of a great enterprise. Do your duty and we cannot fail."

* * *

In the weeks and months that followed nearly everything went according to plan - nearly. Beta Hydri 5, denuded of major portions of its population by plague and exhausted by economic ruin, surrendered completely. Commodore Jadzia received a commendation from the Great Leader for her expedition against Epsilon Eridani 6. Bombardment of that planet never continued beyond the second phase. When the leadership of most of its nations realized the lethality of the Cydonian forces arrayed against them they capitulated immediately.

In the observation lounge of the Battlecruiser Olympus Mons, officers Statler and Waldorf met to exchange friendly banter – and rumors.

"I've read reports that our actions on Beta Hydri 5 and Epsilon Eridani 6 went very well," Statler said.

Waldorf agreed, "Better than hoped for I understand. None of our people suffered so much as a ding on their body armor."

Statler glanced around the room to make sure they were alone, "Have you heard anything about the spy ships?"

"You mean the pathfinder ships b'Eleh and Sorge?"

"Spy ships they were if I remember our last conversation," Statler said.

"Yes I remember. I also remember their mission was very secretive."

Statler bent forward and whispered, "What happened to them is even more secret."

"What?"

"They disappeared," Statler said quietly. "Their disappearance is being kept very quiet."

"What do you mean?"

"I mean they sailed off in pursuit of some warp ship and were never heard from again."

"Nothing at all," Waldorf asked. "Both of them? Perhaps they sent a distress signal over the QC and nobody wants to admit they got into trouble."

"I mean nothing at all has been heard from either spy ship," Statler said. "Nothing arrived over the military QC channels except a single word."

"What word was that," Waldorf asked.

"The word Shundite."

"That's it? That's all? One word? What does Shundite mean?"

"I have no idea," Statler said. "Whatever it means it's got command very rattled."

Chapter 5
INNOCENT'S LAMENT

"History speaks of injustice, but has forgotten how to cry."
– Anna (musician and messenger who died for the Shundite cause on Alpha Cygni Two)

The Great Cydonian Leader, as well as most of the people of his world, began to believe their own propaganda. They came to believe theirs was an exceptional and superior civilization among the family of inhabited planets. They believed they alone possessed the wisdom and ethical standards upon which the people of other worlds ought to live, how they should die and what should be important to them – Cydonian culture. They believed they alone were right to insinuate their hegemony upon others. When their hands seized power and greed filled their hearts the quality of mercy that had been the foundation of Justice on the home world died.

* * *

- Crime and Indifference -

Those who worked in the mines of Alpha Cygni Two were considered chattel – property of the State. Element 92 was the lifeblood of the Empire and Cydonia forced them to dig it out of the living rock.

Prisoners of civil and political crimes were sentenced to work long hours with little rest. They slept in unwarmed barracks. They were offered moldy worm-infested food and because of the scarcity of water often drank their own urine. Those that objected to their treatment or attempted sabotage had iron hooks placed in their necks to punish them as they worked and to prevent them from sleeping.

Many died in the mines of Alpha Cygni Two, but production was unaffected. Other citizens replaced them, arrested for minor infractions of the law. Whispers opposing Cydonian authority earned a death sentence below ground - far from the light of day.

* * *

On Beta Hydri 5 the aftermath of the deadly plague released upon them by the Light Cruiser Chryse had left the indigenous population decimated. The disease had been cured as Cydonian agents promised, but in exchange for renewed health the people lost their freedom of movement on their own world, lost their right to govern themselves and permanently lost the prosperity they'd enjoyed for many years. Public utilities were restricted to an approved elite and common necessities that were once plentiful were rationed.

One day a group of forced laborers were set to work unloading fresh fruit for distribution to the privileged few. Standing nearby was a Cydonian soldier with a whip in one hand and a gun in the other. The delicious aroma of the fruit tantalized the starving workers. Hunger tore at their innards. One young girl who couldn't resist the temptation took a fruit and put it into her mouth.

"It tastes good, doesn't it," the soldier jeered. "I'll give you another one. Open your mouth."

He fired his rifle directly into her mouth splattering her blood and brain matter all over the other workers. No one dared object to the crime. No one ever mentioned it had happened.

* * *

Liberties lost and won over centuries of war between the competing nations of Epsilon Eridani 6 became a lost chapter in its history when the Cydonian heavy Cruisers Sabaea and

Hellas exploded neutron bombs on a few of their small cities. In the wake of overwhelming destructive power that couldn't be challenged, most national capitals surrendered to Cydonian demands. Those that refused to yield disappeared beneath clouds of nuclear fire. Liberties that hadn't been eroded by centuries of war among the inhabitants were completely eliminated during the Cydonian occupation that followed.

A squad of occupying soldiers disembarked from the assault vessel Chaos on the outside of a small city that'd been targeted for neutron irradiation. As they marched toward the city center they passed through the outer edge of the bombs' effective zone and encountered evidence of its' effect upon people and beasts. Farm animals were either dead or screaming from the agony of death's approach. Local inhabitants, who were either dead or were about to die, provided entertainment for jaded Cydonian soldiers.

A young woman, dazed from shock and bleeding heavily from the nose ears and mouth, danced alone next to the dead bodies of her grandmother mother and child. A few of the soldiers broke ranks and danced with her in mockery of her loss.

Further down the road Cydonian troops encountered an old man trapped in a pit of excrement. They stopped and watched as he slowly sank into the mud – screaming for help. No one attempted to help him until nothing remained except a few bubbles where his head had been.

Continuing into the city, soldiers saw an old man lying dead in a pool of blood near a traffic accident caused by the bomb. One arm was missing and each soldier in turn stopped to shake his remaining hand and offer a greeting.

"How are you today? Oh, I see you're dead."

"Smells like something died. Is that you?"

"We're here to take over. Any objections?"

"You shouldn't lie here in the street. You might get hurt," they each said in turn.

* * *

- Lament -

Oh my cities, your names are remembered. You are no more.
Oh my cities, your graceful buildings rise high. No bird nests in your parapets.
Oh my cities, how lonely your streets have become. They once teemed with people.
Oh my cities, you are desolate. Our people are captured into forced labor.
Oh my cities, the Leader has taken our precious things. He mocks our loss.
Oh my cities, our machinery has paused. It waits for the conqueror's evil hand.
Oh my cities, the lament for your passing is bitter.

Nuclear fire has touched our world. Bitter is the day that has seen blood and death. Weep for the naked hills stripped of tall grasses flowers and green trees. Tears hang like a storm over the desolation of our emptiness. Billows of angry dust now swirl where gentle white clouds once danced. Weep for that which has been lost. The torment of our memory is bitter.

Weep for the children who will never know length of days.
Weep for the mothers who gave them birth and know them no more.
Weep for the fathers who dreamed of a future never realized.
Weep for sweet fragrances and delicious aromas traded for the stench of death.
Weep for the dead. Their days among the living are shortened before their time.

Weep for the living. They know only bitterness and suffering.

Much has been lost that was once thought good. Bondage has become our lot. Old memories have soured. Evil times are upon us. It's bitterness scours the heart like hot iron filings. Pain and hunger swallows life in its jaws. Death is our only friend. Our lament is bitter. Our wailing echoes upon empty walls. Our enemy laughs at our tears.

Where is Justice? How did it die? The law is paralyzed and Truth has fled. The wicked have seized us and justice is perverted. A night of despair has fallen. Justice sleeps.

Why has the God of the universe raised up the Cydonians? They are dreaded and feared. From themselves they derive justice and sovereignty. Their warp ships are swifter than light, more powerful than lightning and thunder. They fly like vultures and swoop down to devour. All of them are bent on violence. Their soldiers advance like the wind. They gather prisoners like sand. Why is God silent while the wicked swallow up those more righteous than themselves?

Therefore we must wait for Justice. It will arise like the morning star. The night will flee before its presence. Our punishment will melt away like snow in the rain. Look and see, when Cydonia has accomplished its full measure of evil will the Lord not strike? Like sudden flashes in the sky Judgment will come upon the enemy – even to their utter destruction. At that time the fortunes of the oppressed will be restored. The captives will go free. Justice will prevail.

All will sing for victory and freedom – when Cydonia dies forever before our eyes.

* * *

– Road to Destruction –

Following the successful acquisition of Beta Hydri 5 and Epsilon Eridani 6, expansion of the Empire began to focus upon the methods used to conquer those planets. It had proved easier and quicker to add existing manufacturing power to Cydonian hegemony by means of war and slavery rather than to nurture it for generations among primitive natives. Forced labor camps were normally established to suppress dissent and provide free labor to the corporations that supplied war materials for the Empire. All of it was good for business – evil for humanity.

No one near the Leader objected to the methods used. Even among Cydonian citizens on the home world no one dared to speak against the new policy of militarism. To do so was to risk the loss of possessions they'd gathered unto themselves. Conquest and domination of other worlds was thus established as a quick and easy path to Cydonian prosperity as well as a way to establish the Leader's legacy among the stars.

But what legacy and how long would it last?

* * *

"This war did not come from us. This war came upon us, brought by the sky people of the Great Leader. They came to take our world without a price. On our world they have done much evil. This war came from robbery and slavery and murder. The price of ignominy and injustice will be paid by a war they have begun. It shall be made to visit them."

– T'at'anka Mah'piya (Chief of the Alpha Cygni Two Shundite rebels)

Chapter 6
AMBUSH

"A declaration of war expresses intent. An ambush fulfills it."
- T'at'anka Mah'piya (Chief of the Alpha Cygni Two Shundite rebels)

Warp bubble technology was the ultimate advancement in space travel, allowing any spacecraft equipped with the technology to travel vast distances in a moment of real time. Coincidentally its' vulnerability to attack while en route was significantly reduced. No weapon ever devised could target launch and deliver a lethal warhead at a spacecraft moving through parsecs of the cosmos instantaneously. The impossibility of destroying an object enveloped in a warp bubble changed the nature of war in space.

But it didn't stop it.

* * *

On Alpha Cygni Two the heel of Cydonian colonial authority had pressed upon the necks of its people for nearly three centuries. Holidays had been established, but were nothing more than opportunities for the government to inspire and renew its citizens' allegiance. Flag waving parades, long boring political speeches and time off from work punctuated those observances. Calendars that tracked official Cydonian government holidays, set by a distant government circling a different star, normally listed those days separately.

One particular year an unusual alignment of calendar events would focus attention upon three consecutive days of rest and celebration. Even forced laborers would be allowed to cease their toil for the entire period. That rare congregation of holidays would prove to be an opportune time for an occasion of even greater significance.

Dawn on Dedication Day was hours away when a massive explosion blew half of a Cystapo sub-station into the street. Everyone inside was instantly killed or mortally wounded. An armed assault team charged into the building through billows of choking dust and ash. Dozens of small fires were set as the team searched the building, killed anyone who'd survived the blast, seized official records and destroyed Cystapo QC equipment.

Hundreds of miles away another assault team followed the same pattern when it attacked the main Cystapo office. A team of Shundite rebels entered the building after a large explosive package blew out a sizeable portion of an external rear wall. Anyone who hadn't died in the blast was shot in the head. Inside the building, a few surviving Cystapo agents attempted to defend themselves, but were quickly silenced by small explosives and superior firepower. Rebels entered the QC room and seized equipment used to communicate with Cystapo units on other planets. Before it was disconnected a brief message was sent by the Shundite chief.

Across Alpha Cygni Two violent attacks seized QC centers and silenced ground communication - except for messages sent out by the rebels. Power generation stations were disrupted. Cities across the entire planet went dark. Every police department building in every major and medium size city was attacked and damaged.

At the spaceport a warp ship hauling a load of element 92 ore lifted off and began its ascent toward its interspatial transit point. Before it could reach its optimum altitude three surface to air missiles were launched in its direction. One of the missiles missed the spacecraft entirely. A second one exploded near a trailing edge and caused minor damage, but a third missile struck it in a vital spot. Daylight was minutes away when a huge orange fireball lit the pre-dawn sky above the spaceport. The concussion from the blast smashed windows for a mile in every direction. Flaming wreckage was thrown in all directions as the warp ship plummeted toward the middle of the main aircraft runway. On impact a second explosion again lit the sky as a crater fifty feet wide was blasted into the ground. Aircraft would not be able to use the runway for weeks. Inside the spaceport's main building four armed Shundite rebels broke into the QC room, killed the staff on duty and removed its communications equipment.

The governor's mansion was attacked - first by explosives to gain entry through protective gates and walls and then by several armed teams. Awakened by the noise, the governor sat up in his bed just in time to see several armed men breach the door to his bedroom. His bullet-riddled body was discovered days later along with the corpses of his entire staff. A small private QC room in the residence was denuded of its equipment before the assault team withdrew from the building.

All of these actions were planned and executed on the first day.

* * *

Dedication Day had been established to celebrate the construction of a gigantic stone sculpture of the First Leader. Carved out of a small mountain of solid rock on Cydonia, the edifice resembled the Leader's head. It wore a war helmet and stared with an unblinking resolute gaze into the heavens. For centuries it had stared outward, but because most people had forgotten the First Leader's actual name it was simply called The Face. On Dedication Day everyone in the Cydonian Empire was expected to revere the sculpture as they rested from work and recertified their allegiance to The Great Leader.

The unexpected attacks during the Empire's highest holiday took everyone by surprise. On Phobos Station, Cydonia's principle communication relay center, QC message traffic from Alpha Cygni Two suddenly went quiet. The chief of station assumed it was due to the holiday and didn't notify his superiors of the unusual lack of activity. He would later be reprimanded with the loss of his rank and command responsibilities. Without appeal or review, he would be transferred to the Waste Disposal Division for the remainder of his service period.

* * *

On Alpha Cygni Two, Patriot's Day fell on the second calendar day of holidays. It observed the end of the Shundite revolt several generations earlier. Under the authority of Cystapo Brigadier General Zuph all opposition to Cydonian authority had been suppressed. No apparent resistance had resurfaced since that time, although rumors of its renewal had begun to circulate in recent times. Patriot's Day celebrated unified acceptance of Cydonian authority among the citizenry. This year the celebration would be tainted with open revolt.

News of attacks against Cydonian authority on the previous day spread rapidly across the planet despite damage to its electronic communication channels. Mobs of angry citizens took to the streets in every city to protest Cydonian authority and cruelty. Buildings were vandalized, scores of vehicles were set ablaze and anyone wearing a uniform was brutalized. Fires raged unchecked everywhere. A pall of black smoke, visible from space, hung over the cities. Armed rebels in open roads and on city streets ambushed truckloads of militia rushing to reestablish Cydonian authority. Blood flowed like a river. At the airport/spaceport any craft capable of flight was destroyed or badly damaged. Nothing would take to the skies above Alpha Cygni Two for days.

For reasons only a politician would understand, Lt. Governor Topua declined the honor of assuming the role of governor. Instead, he prevailed upon a judge of the high court to appoint Militia Colonel Capua to that post. Capua was assassinated the next day.

* * *

On the third day, Alpha Cygni Two calendars listed a festival known as Independence Day. Everyone knew it was an artificial holiday because of its dependence upon propaganda slogans rather than anything of substance. Cydonia claimed to inspire liberation from fear of unemployment, ill health and hunger. Despite the slogans many had no work, many suffered untreated ailments and most of the planet starved from rationing. Those that complained soon found themselves with plenty of work in the mines far below ground.

On that auspicious day of true freedom, Shundite rebels attacked the guards of major mining operations and set the captive slave laborers free from their barracks. Many prisoners saw the sky that day for the first time in years. Freed prisoners wept as they walked on soft green grass and sat in the shade of graceful trees eating delicious fruit plucked from their branches. It was a grand end to what came to be called The Three Days of Cleansing, but the best was yet to come.

* * *

Cydonian authorities were slow to react to the QC silence of Alpha Cygni Two. The reasons were several. Some believed a technical glitch was at fault while others suggested the three-day holiday on a planet 600 parsecs distant had led to an understandable but inexcusable slackness on the part of technicians and local leadership. Was everyone up there drunk or asleep?

Dedication Day came and went without a peep from Alpha Cygni Two. Mid-level bureaucrats, who had little real motivation or authority to do their jobs, became concerned. Instead of resolving matters on their own, they passed on their concerns to lower level management. Even on Cydonia the sludge moved downhill.

One of those managers, an enterprising youth with little experience at avoiding unpleasant duties and who worked near the bottom of the bureaucratic ladder, got the bright idea to attempt to contact Defense Minister Rezon personally. T'Alaam's first attempts to contact the Defense Minister failed. Rezon couldn't be reached because he'd absented himself from his government office and apartment in the capital. He'd left Cydonia City to celebrate Dedication Day at his private estate outside the port city of Ortygia Colles on the shore of the Borealis Ocean. T'Alaam made the journey to Rezon's private estate and arrived to find everyone either inebriated or napping.

A guard met the young manager at the gate of Rezon's estate, "what is the nature of your business?"

"It's a matter of state security. It's confidential. I need to speak to Defense Minister Rezon immediately.""

"I'm sorry. I have orders to admit no one," the arrogant guard replied.

In a moment of inspiration, rare among Cydonian bureaucrats, T'Alaam replied that if he wasn't admitted he would return with a squad of Cystapo agents and have the guard shot. The guard opened the gate.

Next in the parade of people who interposed themselves between the Defense Minister and the real world was the estate manager. He was reticent to reveal the location of Rezon. The young bureaucrat repeated the threat he'd used successfully on the gate guard and was rewarded with an escort to Rezon's lanai. The lanai had a beautiful view of the Borealis shore and in a corner of it lay the Defense Minister - asleep in a lounge chair.

"Wake him up, announce my arrival and then leave us alone," T'Alaam ordered.

The house manager did as he was told and left the lanai.

Mentally foggy and half asleep Rezon asked why an insolent young bureaucrat who was working below his pay grade had invaded his home.

"There's a major problem with Alpha Cygni Two, sir. I've come to apprise you of the situation."

Still half asleep the Defense Minister asked what was wrong.

"We don't know, sir. Alpha Cygni Two has gone silent."

"What do you mean they've gone silent?"

"QC channels went silent at the beginning of Dedication Day. We haven't heard from them since."

Rezon sat up, considered the news and shouted for someone to bring him a hot stimulant.

"How long have the QC channels been down?"

T'Alaam shook his head. Hadn't he already passed that information along? He repeated his bad news, "technicians tell us the QC isn't down, sir. They're just silent. They apparently have the ability to respond, but they simply aren't communicating. The channels have been down for three days."

"Has this been verified with Phobos Station?"

"Yes sir. When the channels went silent I talked to them directly. All the information I have comes from Phobos."

The house manager returned with the hot drink Rezon had requested.

"Call my office," the Defense Minister ordered. "If nobody responds call the Leader."

The house manager turned and literally ran into the house to place Rezon's calls.

"Alpha Cygni Two is a problem that has apparently raised its ugly head once again," the Defense Minister said.

"I don't understand sir," the young bureaucrat replied.

"You're too young or too ignorant of Cydonian history. Resistance to our authority seems to be a recurring theme among the inhabitants of that dismal world. The planet is an abundant source of element 92, but also seems to be a garden of insurrection. We shall have to deal with this new problem permanently and harshly."

The house manager returned with a portable phone, "The Leader is on the line, sir."

Rezon stood to his feet and paced back and forth across the lanai as he exchanged words with the Leader. T'Alaam waited patiently. When the conversation between the Leader and Defense Minister ended, Rezon handed the phone back to his house manager.

"I'll be leaving in a few minutes," he said. "A private aircraft is being sent to fetch me back to Cydonia City. You're coming with me young man."

Rezon escorted the young bureaucrat to a private landing zone a few yards from the house, "who is your supervisor?"

T'Alaam told him.

"Why didn't he come here instead of you?"

"I don't know sir. I suppose he was engaged with official duties."

"I know him," Rezon said. "He was probably sick from celebrating too hard."

A high-speed aircraft appeared on the horizon heading in their direction.

"The Leader agrees with my assessment of the situation. You and your supervisor will exchange positions responsibility and pay grade. The Leader has said this decision is effective immediately."

"Thank you, sir."

"Thank the Leader when you see him. He rewards initiative and punishes slackness."

In the absence of communication, silence sounded an alarm of exceptional intensity. Speculation wasn't one of the guiding principles of the Cydonian Empire, so Defense Minister Rezon decided to order a troop of soldiers to Alpha Cygni Two to teach them a lesson in protocol. It was thought two warp ships would be adequate to the task. Preparations were begun immediately. If deliberate negligence was discovered, the military commander was authorized to arrest and replace those responsible.

A troop transport of the same type that had been used to attack Epsilon Eridani 6 was assigned the mission. Accompanying the transport spacecraft was the Light Cruiser Chryse, commanded by Commodore T'Sha. T'Sha had been promoted following his successful covert operation on Beta Hydri 5 several years earlier. Several days were required to muster and equip the soldiers before they could board their warp transport for the journey to Alpha Cygni Two.

Nobody on that silent planet was asleep or inebriated. Quite a few were preparing for what they knew would be an important encounter with the Cydonian military. No one neglected preparations for an imminent visit in force. Surprises from Alpha Cygni Two had not yet ended.

* * *

If confidence and arrogance were fuel, Commodore T'Sha wouldn't have needed element 92 to power his spacecraft. Blinded by its own pride the crew of the light cruiser Chryse and its escort, the assault ship Terror, lifted off from the new Cydonian spaceport at Tempe Terra. Watching from Sacra Mensa ridge overlooking the plain below was a newly appointed mid-level supervisor from the Defense Ministry. A sense of unease pervaded his mind and as the warp ships approached the interspatial transit point T'Alaam wrote a memo to Defense Minister Rezon. In his memo he revealed personal reservations about the upcoming mission, but admitted he had nothing to go on but a gut feeling. Rezon replied by advising him to take an antacid to cure his gut feeling.

* * *

Light cruiser Chryse and assault ship Terror reentered normal space above Alpha Cygni Two and assumed a low orbit. Shortly after stabilizing their trajectory a large number of objects appeared on short-range sensors heading in their general direction.

"Send a brief message to Phobos Station via QC," Commodore T'Sha told his Communication officer. "Tell them we've established a standard orbit and are preparing for ground assault."

"Yes, sir. It's on the way."

"While you're connected tell them we're tracking an inbound reception party. Thank them for the courtesy."

"Yes, sir. Right away, sir."

Chryse's Combat Data Center contacted Commodore T'Sha and advised him the configuration of the approaching vessels wasn't registered on their database.

"Perhaps they're a new design from one of our outer colonies," T'Sha speculated.

His words would prove to be the last ones uttered during peacetime.

When the approaching vessels came within close proximity they opened fire on the Chryse with heavy energy weapons. A small number broke off from the main body and attacked the Terror. Huge gaps were ripped open in the Chryse's hull, disabling the Life Support section. Unwitting crew were sucked into space along with all manner of loose bits of metal and paper. The Terror was hit in the cargo compartment, which on that mission was providing accommodations for Cydonian soldiers. Everyone in that compartment died from exposure to the vacuum and cold of space.

"Send an emergency message to Phobos via QC," T'Sha ordered his Communication officer. "Tell them we're under attack by unknown spacecraft. We're severely damaged. Life support is failing. The Terror was hit in the cargo section. Conditions there are unknown to us."

Neither Chryse nor Terror was able to return fire upon their assailants.

In their arrogance and pride, the Cydonian Space Service had assumed theirs was the only space faring civilization in the universe. It was believed no other civilization was capable of warp bubble travel and no other civilization could develop high capacity energy weapons for use in space combat. As a consequence of their oversight, Chryse mounted only air to surface missile systems and gravity bombs. Those weapons were designed for ground targets within atmosphere. Neither could be used as a defense from attack in space. Terror carried no weapon systems at all. Both Chryse and Terror were helpless to resist their attackers.

"Commodore T'Sha, I'm receiving a message from the attackers by standard radio frequency," the Communications officer of the Chryse reported.

"Put it on audio," T'Sha said.

"This is Admiral Talako of the Shundite Alliance. You are ordered to surrender your two spacecraft immediately. Heave to and prepare to be boarded."

T'Sha asked his attackers to identify themselves, "Who's the Shundite Alliance?"

"We're the ones that'll blow you to bits if you don't comply with our orders," Talako answered. "You cannot fight and you cannot escape. Surrender or die."

* * *

On Phobos Station the radioman on duty punched the alert signal. Red lights flashed everywhere on the station. The harsh whine of the war claxon announced a real battle situation for the first time in the history of the Space Service. On Cydonia, similar warnings were duplicated in the War Room.

The Chief of Station burst into the observation chamber and screamed at the radioman, "What's going on? Why did you sound the alarm?"

"Look at this message," the radioman said.

The Chief's hand began to shake when he read the high priority dispatch, "Send this to Space Service Command immediately."

"Already done, Chief."

* * *

T'Alaam entered the office of the Defense Minister, "You called, Minister Rezon?"

"I apologize for calling you out in the middle of the night, but a situation has arisen I believe you need to hear about."

"Situation, sir?"

"Read this dispatch."

Rezon handed a single sheet of paper to Manager T'Alaam. The word 'secret' was stenciled in red letters across its letterhead. Deep furrows appeared on T'Alaam's brow as he read it.

"How long ago did this happen," T'Alaam asked.

"We believe it happened as soon as Chryse and Terror dropped into normal space above Alpha Cygni Two. Our best guess is that the dispatch is two to three hours old."

"Has anything been heard from either spacecraft since that time?"

"No and nothing has been heard from that planet either. All are as silent as a grave."

T'Alaam handed the paper back to Rezon, "who or what is the Shundite Alliance?"

"Nobody here knows. Our intelligence section believes they may be associated with the Shundite rebels."

"Those people obviously have access to warp bubble technology. How could they have acquired it," T'Alaam asked.

"What I'm about to tell you is classified information. You're not to discuss this with anyone outside this office or anyone I haven't authorized. Do you understand?"

"Yes, sir."

"Under the leadership of Cystapo Brigadier General Zuph a rebellion on Alpha Cygni Two was suppressed."

"I'm familiar with history, sir. It was a long time ago if I remember correctly – a rather minor insurrection."

"Nothing about it was minor. Mining and transport of element 92 had been interdicted to the point that nearly all shipments were shut down. The Leader sent General Zuph to Alpha Cygni Two to put an end to the resistance. During that rebellion a warp transport spacecraft was hijacked."

"If the hijacking is classified, then may I ask who took it? Where did it go, sir?"

"We never learned where it was taken, but Shundite rebels were responsible."

"We lost a warp transport to a group of rebels? I've never heard of that happening."

"Nobody has and nobody will if this information remains secret."

"Don't you think that's a minor point, Minister Rezon? A hostile group now has warp technology. Those same people have demonstrated the ability to capture or destroy two of our best spacecraft. What other technology have they stolen that we don't know about?"

"We don't know."

"With all due respect sir, we seem to be standing on the threshold of an interstellar war. There's too much about our enemy we don't know and too much they appear to know about us."

"Unfortunately that's about all that's known for certain. There's one more thing you need to know."

"What's that, sir?"

"You are now promoted to Deputy Defense Minister. Any time you have a gut feeling about something you're to use your new authority to do something about it."

"Thank you, sir. Do I have the Leader to thank for my promotion?"

"No. This time it's on me. Bear in mind you can lose your position as quickly as you gained it."

"Thank you again, sir. What are we going to do about this situation?"

"Nobody knows, Deputy T'Alaam. It's the middle of the night outside and everybody on the inside is in the dark. Nobody knows."

Supremely confident in its superiority, Cydonian leadership was truly rattled by events on Alpha Cygni Two. Confusion ruled the minds of leadership. Finger pointing and accusations of guilt began to be a preoccupation of those who coveted power. The first large crack in the edifice of the empire had appeared. There would soon be others.

Chapter 7
WAR

"It is typical of Cydonia to deny the superiority of any world but their own."
T'at'anka Mah'piya

The war was fought in a thousand places hundreds of parsecs apart. It was fought for reasons important to some and barely understood by others. It was fought by worlds that had never known the existence of other civilizations and by societies so old their knowledge of inhabited planets existed in dusty volumes of interstellar antiquity. It was fought by heroes and by cowards. It was fought by vast armies and by individual soldiers slogging through the mud of the wreck and ruin of war. It was fought by fleets of spacecraft struggling in sterile space over lines of supply, guarding the gateways to planetary invasion slavery and death.

Like most wars, the tempo of the conflict between the Cydonian Star Empire and the Shundite Alliance began slowly. As months became years its intensity increased, expanding beyond its original boundaries to affect many worlds not previously engaged. It culminated in a life and death struggle unforeseen by Cydonian leaders who had taken up arms against innocent peaceful people.

It was Cydonia who taught the value of life and the meaning of liberty by stealing it. It was the Cydonian Star Empire that taught its' enemies the meaning of vengeance. It was from Cydonia, the harbinger of war, that a terrible awful bloody lesson was learned - that ultimate victory required nothing less than decisive total and absolute annihilation. Upon the challenge issued by the Cydonian Star Empire, accepted by the Shundite Alliance, would the future of an untold number of worlds depend.

An entire library could not hold the chronicles of all those who fought an ancient war between the stars. These are a few of their stories.

* * *

Billows of acrid smoke poured out of long gashes in the fuselage of Assault Ship Sword as it plummeted toward the unforgiving planet below. A single fighter of the Shundite Alliance followed close behind – continuing to fire its weapons in an attempt to cause further damage. When the fatally wounded spacecraft entered atmosphere and began to burn from friction, the fighter broke off pursuit. In doing so the Shundite flier allowed its targets' skilled pilots some latitude in their efforts to prevent a crash that might otherwise have been fatal to all aboard.

The Cydonian vessel bellied into an ungraceful landing, causing major damage to what remained of its hull. On contact with the ground, the flaming spacecraft burst open like an overcooked potato in a microwave oven. Smoke and fire engulfed the dying craft as its passengers and crew scrambled into the fresh air - racing for cover from fear of an explosion. Assault Ship Sword would never take to the sky again.

Cydonian High Command hadn't considered the ambush at Alpha Cygni Two a serious threat to continued expansion of the Empire. Consequently its subordinate commanders weren't warned of possible resistance to their assigned tasks elsewhere. The invasion of Beta Hydri 7 would prove to be a bitter fruit of that negligence.

Instead of adopting appropriate cautions, Commodore Jadzia proudly marched onto the bridge of Heavy Cruiser Cimmeria confident in the assumption her plans would lead to another success for the Empire. Her plan was similar to the campaign she'd successfully conducted against Epsilon Eridani 6 and for which she'd been awarded a commendation from the Leader himself. A barrage of neutron bombs targeting small cities would be followed by a ground assault intended to seize communications centers and disrupt transportation.

Her logistics were perfect. Troops and spacecraft crews under her command were seasoned and well trained. She had twice the number of soldiers as on the previous occasion. This time, however, the fortunes of war would not smile upon her plans for Beta Hydri 7.

Events that day were confused from the beginning and shocking at the end. Commodore Jadzia stood on the bridge of her command ship and pondered the loss of Assault Ship Hammer a few hours earlier. Its sister ship Sword no longer responded via QC or standard radio frequencies. Prior to their disappearance, both ships reported being attacked by Shundite fighters. This was not part of her battle plan against Beta Hydri 7.

Jadzia petted the commendation medal hanging on her uniform as she pondered the meaning of a report from Light Cruiser Sirenum describing a brief assault upon its orbital position. Enemy fighters appeared out of nowhere, caused minor damage, broke off their brief attack and withdrew. With the loss of half her spacecraft and damage to one of her remaining cruisers, Jadzia ordered a withdrawal to Cydonia as soon as practicable. She would have some explaining to do when she reached the home world and she knew she would not have a sympathetic audience. The invasion of Beta Hydri 7 had failed.

* * *

War correspondent Aletheia struggled through a field of mud as she approached the scene of a recent battle.

"I don't remember the name of this planet or the star it circles," she wrote. "It's so far from the edge of Cydonian influence I doubt anyone on the home world has heard of it or even knows we're here.

Why are we here?

That's one of the questions a journalist ought to propose, but no one I've met seems to be able to answer it."

The smell of death arrived on the wind long before she saw evidence of the battle. Aletheia gagged from the stench, reached into her haversack and pulled out a small bottle of odor resistant gel. She held her breath while she applied it under her nose – hoping it would give some relief from the awful reek.

"Carrion birds are wheeling in the air," she noted. "The battlefield must be beyond the next rise in the ground."

A minor respite from the clinging mud accompanied her ascent to the top of the small hill before her. When she reached its summit she paused to survey the view ahead. Dead men and wrecked machinery littered the ground as far as the eye could see. Beyond were the outer boundaries of the planet's only spaceport. The goal of the battle had been to win its possession.

Aletheia continued down the far side of the hill and stepped onto the battlefield. It was plain to see how the fight had gone by the way the dead bodies were arranged. The story was all laid out on the ground for her and the birds to appreciate. Each in their separate way feasted upon the field of death at their feet.

Some of the dead soldiers lay alone in the field's high grass. Others lay in groups. Bits and pieces of paper blew across the field driven by an afternoon breeze. She picked up several. Each of them appeared to be personal. Some of the papers were photographs from happier times – smiling families, sports teams all young and strong, an attractive mate in a winsome pose, and sometimes a baby or beloved pet. All were from home wherever home happened to be. All the soldiers, regardless of whatever uniform they wore, had their pockets turned inside out.

"Pick pockets of the dead have already scoured the battlefield," Aletheia wrote in her notebook. "Rats, or the equivalent form of that animal on this planet, have already been at work chewing out the eyes of the corpses."

Carrion birds squawked at each other as they claimed the best meat. Others hopped into the air as Aletheia walked past their gruesome work. The wind blew more papers across her path.

"A lot of war material is scattered throughout the field," she wrote. "Some of it is bright and new as though it had just come from the factory. Most of it is in bits – broken, twisted, burned and distorted into unrecognizable shapes. Always there are papers blowing around.

There are haversacks, metal cases of all shapes and sizes, bits of torn clothing ripped off the bodies of their owners by the impact of some weapon or bomb. There are knives and small digging tools, hand held things that look like small bombs or grenades, medical kits and open wallets next to the pockets pulled inside out. And the wind carries papers over and around it all."

In several places were larger pieces of equipment twisted in odd shapes by chemical explosions or melted by concentrated fire from energy weapons. Aletheia guessed they'd been guns or vehicles. Some of them were pointed toward the spaceport. Others pointed away from it, as though defending it from advancing troops. Bloated bodies near the guns had died in various positions of operating the equipment. Other bodies seemed to have been surprised by death - caught unaware by a sudden attack.

"Many of the bodies have no arms or legs, but the missing parts are nowhere to be found," Aletheia wrote. "Perhaps carrion feeding animals have taken the body parts to another location. Older bodies are swollen and bloated. The newer dead lay as though asleep, but always their pockets are inside out. Everywhere there are papers."

Far away on her right Aletheia saw a vague figure picking its way among the detritus of war. On her left another figure did the same. She called to one, who ran away from the sound of her voice. Aletheia approached the boundary of the spaceport, which had at one time been protected by a wire-linked fence topped by cutting wire. The fence had been knocked down in several places. Aletheia stepped through.

Hidden in a building on the perimeter of the spaceport was a soldier whose task it was to guard against infiltrators. He'd been watching a solitary figure as it picked its way across the battlefield. When the individual crossed the fence line he took aim and fired. The figure was hit squarely on target. The body dropped to the ground on his first shot and remained motionless. A number of papers it had been holding in its hand were released - all swept away by the wind to join the multitude of other papers strewn everywhere across the battlefield.

* * *

Clouds of war were heavy and oppressive everywhere in the Empire, but on Cydonia gullible citizens and their corrupt leaders went about their daily lives confident in their delusion that all was well. Electronic and print media headlined the antics of public celebrities and scandalous affairs of low-level politicians for the purpose of public consumption. Sports tournaments were the objects of obsessive attention. Millions memorized team scores and winning performances from one season to the next. Media giants treated stories of never ending criminal behavior and personal tragedy as light entertainment. Momentous issues were trivialized and obvious ones were complicated to the point of incredulity. Nobody concerned themselves with the fate of millions of people who lived on other worlds and had been made slaves of the Empire – or worse, had died because of it.

Chronicles of the continued expansion of the Empire were published in the driest most uninteresting prose possible. The general population, more or less bored with continual success, paid little attention. Boasts that the Empire presently encompassed several hundred worlds, all under the authoritarian rule of the Leader and his appointed governors, fell on ears dulled with constant repetitious slogans and clichés.

A news release issued by the Cydonian Ministry of Defense appeared on seldom-read pages of the print media - opposite the daily cross word puzzle. The story quoted Deputy Defense Minister T-Alaam's announcement of an attack by forces of the Shundite Alliance upon a defenseless passenger transport near Beta Hydri 7. It was deceptive, but it was good press.

* * *

Hundreds of feet below ground near the Cydonian capital city, a huge complex of government offices, apartments, science labs, shops, restaurants and even a power station was carved out of living rock. Above it all at ground level was raised a five-sided pyramid so large it could be seen clearly from orbit. As a consequence of its geometric shape it was called the Pentagon Pyramid.

Inside the Pentagon, far below ground level, a few in positions of authority were called to the private war room of the Leader. The purpose of the meeting was to identify problems and discuss solutions created by the Shundite Alliance.

"The first issue on my agenda is to ask who these people are," the Leader announced. "Who or what is the Shundite Alliance?"

"If I may be allowed to begin," Defense Minister Rezon explained. "The Shundite Alliance seems to have originated during the rebellion on Alpha Cygni Two. We assumed it had been suppressed by General Zuph and the Cystapo."

The Leader SLAMMED his fist on the table, "Do you think I'm an idiot, Minister Rezon? I know about the Shundite rebellion. Are you unaware of my ability to read classified reports?"

"I apologize My Leader. I only meant to review the history of the movement."

"I KNOW the history, Rezon. What I have never learned and still don't know is what happened to the warp transport hijacked from Alpha Cygni Two. Who is responsible for these attacks against our vassal worlds? I'm repeating old questions here because no one has offered any answers. Where did the warp transport go? Who or what is the Shundite? Does anyone know?"

"With all due respect My Leader," Cystapo Deputy Intelligence Minister Baishan said. "We've employed every device and method at our disposal to learn the answer to those critical questions. To date we've learned nothing about the destination of the hijacked spacecraft. It can only be assumed it was examined by those who could reverse engineer our technology."

The Leader pulled a handgun out of a holster at his waist and pointed it squarely at Baishan's head, "I will hear no more echoes of information I already know. Tell me something I don't know or you will surely die right here and right now. I didn't call this meeting to waste time on history lessons."

"My apologies," Baishan said coldly. "I have no way of knowing what you know or what you don't know. I don't sit next to you looking over your shoulder when you read reports about them."

The Leader put his gun down on the table. Everyone politely waited for his next words.

"I know pathfinder ships b'Eleh and Sorge were assigned the mission of following a warp trail to the destination of the hijacked transport," the Leader said. "I also know they never returned and that their one word final message suggested the Shundite were responsible for their loss. Is it possible to repeat that search?"

"Not at this time," Rezon admitted. "A warp bubble signature disperses rather quickly. Despite the sensitivity of our instruments the trail has gone cold. However, we may not have to follow the same path to learn the location of a member planet of the Shundite Alliance. It's my contention there's no actual Shundite home world to discover in the first place."

"What do you mean?"

"Our enemy calls itself the Shundite Alliance," Rezon said. "We know this because Shundite Admiral Talako identified himself to Commodore T'Sha just before T'Sha surrendered his spacecraft."

"I'm aware of that unfortunate episode," the Leader said. His hand moved to the top of the table and rested on his gun, "Tell me something I don't know."

Tension among those seated at the table became so thick a knife could almost cut it. Deputy Minister Baishan wondered privately who would be shot first – Rezon or himself.

Rezon continued as calmly as though he were trading dinner recipes with his relatives, "If we assume Admiral Talako's reference to an alliance of the Shundite is true, then we may also assume two or more worlds have conspired to make war upon the Empire instead of just one. Efforts to find a single planet directing efforts against us may be a fruitless waste of time and resources."

The Leader removed his hand from the gun, "Do you have any suggestions as to how we may proceed, Minister Rezon?"

"I do, sir. I propose we make available a flotilla of heavily armed spacecraft for the purpose of assaulting a Shundite base of operations. We may learn much from captured Alliance personnel and Shundite documents. When we do, we'll be better able to carry the fight to them."

"How do you suggest we go about finding this hidden Shundite base," The Leader asked.

"I don't. We let them find us."

"Are you suggesting we dangle bait in space," the Leader asked. "When they come to us and take the bait we then follow them back to their base. Is that your plan?"

"Exactly right, sir."

"What do we use as bait," The Leader asked. "Where in all of Cydonian controlled space should we put it?"

"Your last question first," Minister Rezon said as he heaved a pile of documents onto the conference table. "This is a list of attacks and raids against assets of the Empire. It's rather extensive, but in the interest of time I'll restrict my review to a few of the more interesting incidents."

"Why is your list interesting," one of the older men at the table asked. "Any attack against us is a violation of our sovereignty and authority. Such attacks are hardly interesting."

"They are if we mean to put an end to them," Minister Rezon replied. "In the past two years the number of raids and attacks against us has increased in number in ferocity and in the amount of damage they cause. Whether we want to admit it or not we have a war on our hands."

"I agree with your assessment of the situation," the Leader acknowledged. "We are certainly at war. Please continue with your presentation Minister Rezon."

"What my analysts have found interesting is that the most severe of these attacks have been spatially close to our own world. At first we assumed a base of the Shundite Alliance would have been further away. Today the statistics we've compiled suggest otherwise."

"What data are you using to establish your assumption?"

"Alpha Cygni Two was the point of departure for the hijacked warp transport. We've always guessed the spacecraft's destination might have been closer to that planet - six hundred parsecs away from us. On the other hand, the highest number of actual documented attacks and raids has been much closer to Cydonia than to Alpha Cygni Two. Statistics indicate conclusions our guesses did not. Allow me to read a few report summaries for you.

In the region of Alpha Aquilae, five parsecs distant from Cydonia, more than a dozen raids and ambushes upon fuel extraction plants and military bases have been reported.

A new colony on Alpha Lyrae, eight parsecs away, has been raided five times. There are no developed industries on that world other than those supporting the colonists.

Our Vega colony, eight parsecs distant, was massacred. Every last man woman and child was either killed or abducted. We have only fragmented records of the attack, but those we gleaned from the ruins identified the Shundite Alliance as the responsible party.

At Wolf 359, two point six parsecs from us, over forty raids and attacks upon transport spacecraft and ground based factories have been reported in the last half-year alone. Last year a pathfinder spacecraft engaged and severely damaged an enemy fighter. Our pathfinder ship sustained heavy damage itself, but was able to drive the Shundite spacecraft away. Because of the recent increase in raids we've stationed a squadron of our new interceptors there. Our engagements with Shundite fighters have been successful in terms of defending our ground installations, but our interceptors have suffered heavy losses.

At Reticuli Z2 on planet LV426, twelve parsecs away from our Home World, one raid attacked an element 92 processing plant. Ground based defenses were able to drive away the single enemy spacecraft before serious damage was inflicted.

Oddly, there are two locations with large established colonies and productive processing facilities that have not been attacked at all. We manage three untouched planets in the 61 Virginis star system twenty-seven parsecs away and two more in the Kappa Ceti system about one hundred point six parsecs from Cydonia.

Of all the star systems we've considered as Shundite bases of operation, two are of high interest to us. They are star systems V2500 and KIC 8462852."

"Why are they interesting?"

"V2500 is the oldest known star system and is only three parsecs away. We're interested in it because it's closest to points we've suffered attack. KIC 8462852 is four hundred fifty parsecs away. We're looking at that one because it's closest to the original theory about the destination of the hijacked warp transport and because it demonstrates very anomalous astronomical behavior. Data from both star systems is incomplete because we've never received information from any probe sent to either of them.

I can read dozens of additional reports all documenting gradually intensified activity against us, but the ones I just outlined stand out in stark relief. Somewhere in all this information is a place we can engage the enemy with hope of learning something new about them."

"Wolf 359," The Leader said.

"The numbers agree with you, sir," Defense Minister Rezon said. "I also believe Wolf 359 is where we should dangle our bait."

The Leader reminded Rezon of his first question, "What do we use as bait?"

Rezon smiled, "You, sir."

Baishan put his head in his hands and prepared to hear a gunshot. A few moments later he dared a glance at the Leader. The man was smiling and nodding as though he'd just heard the best joke of his life.

* * *

An exciting and rare news story broke on every media outlet of the Cydonian Star Empire. People on every planet, outpost, monitoring station and spacecraft were made aware of the incredible event. On Dedication Day The Great Leader would personally present awards commendations and accolades for outstanding accomplishments in production defense and research to citizens of a new colony world.

"Our Great Leader has never traveled beyond Cydonia," one commentator breathlessly announced to his audience. "This year he'll be acknowledging the achievements of citizens of the Empire when he journeys to planet 5 of the Wolf 359 star system."

* * *

On Dedication Day, video panels throughout the Empire allowed every citizen the opportunity to watch their Great Leader march solemnly toward a warp transport at the Tempe Terra spaceport on Cydonia.

A commentator's voice described what viewers could plainly see for themselves, "Our Leader is resplendent in a gold helmet and dark green uniform accessorized with items of gold and silver. He appears to be carrying a satchel we believe to contain medals and award certificates to be presented later today on Wolf 359. Our citizens on that nearby star system are extremely excited about his visit. All of us envy their opportunity to see the Leader in person. We have reports that thousands of people are lining the parade route from the Wolf 359 spaceport to the award venue. Our normal Dedication Day programming will have a special significance today when we cover this momentous event in history."

The figure that had marched across the tarmac and boarded the transport was seated and strapped into its chair. Wires connecting its wrist to a battery pack in the satchel it carried were disconnected and replaced with a direct connection to the transport's power system. Batteries inside the satchel were connected to the transport's power system for recharging. A short coded message was sent by the spacecraft pilot directly to the war room at the Pentagon and was acknowledged by one of the three people sitting in the darkened chamber.

Cameras watched as The Leader's transport lifted into the atmosphere. It glowed brightly as it approached its interspatial transit point, circled a few times and disappeared. Commentators described the routine procedure to viewers who eagerly waited and watched for the Leader's arrival at Wolf 359.

* * *

Shundite fighters seemed to appear out of nowhere as the Leader's warp transport and its escort Pathfinder-73 re-entered normal space above planet 5 of the Wolf 359 system. A short message sent by standard radio frequency from the transport pilot notified receiving stations on the planet below that enemy spacecraft had been sighted.

"Enemy approaching on an intercept vector," the pilot reported. "Spacecraft identified as ten standard Shundite fighters. Sensors report they're charging their energy weapons. Beginning evasive maneuvers."

Two Cydonian interceptors resolved into normal space and assumed positions on each side of the transport. Pathfinder-73 withdrew to a position five hundred miles behind its' three larger companions. Moments later, Shundite fighters commenced firing with long-range energy bursts each of which passed very close to the transport spacecraft.

Shundite attackers formed into five groups of two fighters each and hurled themselves toward the transport. Its' pilot tried to alter the spacecraft's position in space, but it was like trying to move an asteroid with a can of compressed air. The transport hadn't been designed for violent abrupt course changes.

Pilot procedures had been clearly assigned for this particular mission. Following his limited efforts to save the vessel the pilot pressurized his space suit, shut down all life support systems and entered an armored escape pod.

Distances separating Shundite fighter groups from the Cydonian transport narrowed quickly, allowing their energy weapons to pepper the transport's hull with ever more accurate fire. Cydonian interceptors, more agile and faster than Shundite fighters, split off and attacked two separate groups. Pathfinder-73 retreated further and energized its warp bubble engines.

Each Cydonian interceptor immediately destroyed one Shundite fighter and damaged the other in the paired groups they attacked, but doing so was difficult and time consuming. Though Shundite fighters were slower and less maneuverable in space, their weapons were much more powerful. Fighter spacecraft were difficult to damage. Cydonian interceptors were more agile and harder to target.

Shundite fighters took to space with shielding around the spacecraft engine and pilot compartment. Cydonian interceptors were faster and more maneuverable because they had no armor at all. Interceptor weapons were less powerful, but more accurate. One hit fired by a Shundite fighter could disable or destroy a Cydonian interceptor, while it took several hits to inflict the same amount of damage on a Shundite fighter. Outnumbered and outgunned the more maneuverable Cydonian interceptors were unable to provide the protection they'd hoped.

The Cydonian transport carrying its robotic leader figure had been fitted with protective armor before it began its mission, but the shielding afforded little protection against six Shundite fighters now closing for the kill. Twenty Cydonian interceptors were scrambling through the atmosphere at incredible speed, but were still seconds away from the scene of battle. Fatal shots fired by the nearest Shundite fighters struck the transport's engine compartment causing internal explosions that ripped the transport into two separate pieces.

Four of the remaining six Shundite fighters broke off their attack upon the dead transport and turned their attention upon the interceptors. In the melee that followed one of them was destroyed and the other badly damaged. One fighter that had been hit several times began to drift in space. Believing they'd accomplished their mission, the remaining Shundite raiders engaged their warp bubbles and disappeared from the spreading wreckage they'd caused. As they withdrew from the battle Pathfinder-73 followed in their wake. Two and a half parsecs away a small crowd gathered in the Pentagon war room to learn the results of the engagement. They weren't disappointed when a coded message was received via QC circuit from Pathfinder-73.

"This is exactly what we'd hoped for," the Leader declared. "Order our fleet to attack the target planet at V2500."

"Order issued My Leader," Minister Rezon reported. "Our fleet is on its way.

Scattered wreckage and a rescue beacon from the surviving Cydonian interceptor were all that greeted the rescue group when they arrived from the planet's surface. Five Shundite fighters had been destroyed. Only one Cydonian interceptor pilot had died when his Shundite opponent blasted his ship. The transport pilot was alive and well in his escape pod when he was picked up drifting in space. The robotic duplicate of the Leader would need a new battery and a paint job.

* * *

"There are millions of people waiting to see you on the parade route at Wolf 359," Deputy Minister Baishan said. "They're going to be very disappointed. What are we going to tell them?"

"Tell them the truth," the Leader said. "Tell them the Shundite Alliance attacked my ship above planet 5. Tell them I suffered no injury from the attack. Tell them I'm alive and well and will address them via videoconference link later today."

The leader sat back in his chair and folded his arms, "Perhaps we'll have good news to share from V2500 as well. I'll enjoy adding that to my usual Dedication Day speech."

Chapter 8
TURNING POINT

Like a faithful hunting dog, Pathfinder-73 used its electronic sensors to follow Shundite fighters to their base after the Wolf 359 raid. Speculation among those in the Leader's inner circle of counselors assumed V2500 was the most likely point of origin for Shundite activity, but a major military offensive couldn't be based on guesses - as educated as they might have been. The little spacecraft put an end to everyone's theories when it transmitted hard evidence back to waiting eyes and ears in the Pentagon war room. The discovery was gratifying, but not altogether unexpected.

Proof the attack had come from the V2500 star system also included the location of the planet used as a Shundite base of operations. Identified as Kana on Cydonian star charts, the planet radiated so many warp traces it couldn't have been interpreted as anything other than an enemy base of operations. The Leader responded by ordering an immediate attack upon Kana by every available Cydonian spacecraft.

* * *

Sidron Kuza wasn't born on Cydonia. Like many of the officers in the Space Service he'd spent his youth as a service brat. Both his parents were officers and he'd traveled with them from planet to planet whenever their duty assignments changed. He enjoyed playing organized games and made friends easily, especially when the other kids realized he had a talent for winning.

Sidron was eleven years old when his mother died in a reactor accident. A year later his father sent him to a military school on Cydonia where he took to its life of discipline like a fish takes to water. He was a likeable fellow and had a genius for leadership. Frequently voted captain of his sporting squads, he drilled his teams hard and never lost a competition. Upon graduation from military school he entered Space Service Academy where he received top honors in his class and not one single demerit.

Awards and achievements during service in the fleet accumulated rapidly. Some thought the universe smiled on him as it did few others. As a young lieutenant fresh out of the Academy, he achieved his first commendation when he rescued his commanding officer from almost certain death at the hands of a group of mutineers. A unit citation for efficiency was awarded his first command of a pathfinder spacecraft followed in quick succession by a series of promotions resulting from successful actions against Shundite raiders. Sidron Kuza knew how to get results.

When orders were issued to assemble all available spacecraft for action against the Shundite Alliance at V2500, the Leader's first act was to draft a promising officer to lead them. Kuza's reputation as a winner had preceded him and it came as no surprise to anyone in Space Service to hear he'd been asked to assume that responsibility.

Fleet Admiral Kuza organized his spacecraft into two fleets for the attack against Kana. He would command the First Fleet and Vice Admiral Maur would be responsible for the Second Fleet. Warp engines were engaged and the spacecraft of the Cydonian Star Empire sailed into history.

* * *

From the beginning of the operation, nothing went according to plan. When Admiral Kuza's First Fleet dropped out of warp near Kana, the Shundite Alliance was ready for him. Already in position and on alert to repel an attack, Shundite forces weren't taken by surprise as everyone in the Leader's entourage had hoped.

Kuza barely had time to organize his spacecraft in a defensive formation before First Fleet came under heavy Shundite attack. The Fleet Admiral sent an emergency QC message to Vice Admiral Maur prior to his planned arrival with Second Fleet.

FROM: FLEET 1
V2500 STAR SYSTEM OPERATIONS
BATTLECRUISER OLYMPUS MONS 022421FASK
FLEET ADMIRAL SIDRON KUZA, COMMANDING

TO: FLEET 2
LIGHT CRUISER SIRENUM 022421VALM
VICE ADMIRAL LITHOS MAUR, COMMANDING

ALERT BULLETIN

IMPERATIVE YOU ABORT OUR BATTLE PLAN REGARDING YOUR ARRIVAL HERE WITH SECOND FLEET. I AM UNDER HEAVY ATTACK.

SEVERAL INTERCEPTORS ALREADY LOST.
BATTLECRUISER OLYMPUS MONS IS TAKING HEAVY FIRE WITH LIGHT DAMAGE.
HEAVY CRUISER CIMMERIA SUSTAINED HEAVY FIRE WITH MODERATE DAMAGE.
FRIGATE ERYTHRAEM DESTROYED.
FRIGATE LACUS BADLY DAMAGED.

FIRST FLEET STILL BATTLE-WORTHY.

A NEW BATTLE PLAN IS TO BE IMPLEMENTED IMMEDIATELY.

INITIATE ENCRYPTED VIDEO CONFERENCE WITH ME AS SOON AS PRACTICABLE.

THIS IS A BATTLE ALERT.

-30-

QC TRANSCRIPTION V2500-1 ### WJ7121

Almost as soon as his QC message was sent, Admiral Kuza received a request to accept an encrypted videoconference call from Vice Admiral Maur.

Maur appeared on Admiral Kuza's video screen, "I read you are heavily engaged with the enemy, sir. What do you need from us?"

"Shundite forces opposing us are approximately twice the combined number of First and Second Fleet. We have lost the element of surprise. I don't believe we can engage them in our present configuration with any reasonable hope of success."

"Do you wish to withdraw," Maur asked.

"Negative. I'm hoping to reestablish the initiative we'd hoped for from the beginning. I intend to surprise them."

"If you are already engaged with the enemy how are you going to surprise them?"

"I'm not. You and Second Fleet will surprise them."

"The idea sounds promising, Admiral. How do you wish to proceed?"

"I'm going to detach a large number of spacecraft from my fleet and order them to join Second Fleet under your command. There's a good chance the Alliance won't detect the warp transfer. If they do see spacecraft leaving my formation they may assume I'm retreating. Individual unit orders will be issued as soon as this communication is terminated. Your combined force will be approximately two-thirds our entire strength."

"Protocol suggests you strengthen your position in the face of a superior enemy, not weaken it," Maur cautioned.

"The Shundite Alliance knows battle protocol as well as we do. I'm hoping they'll see the weakening of First Fleet and interpret it as a retreat or preparation for general warp withdrawal. If I'm correct they'll call up their reserves and press the attack against me. When that happens their rear area will be exposed to your surprise attack."

"Incredible idea, sir. It may work if it's done quickly."

"We don't have time for anything other than quick action. This must be done rapidly if it's to succeed at all."

"Very well. What are your orders, Admiral?"

"You are to order Second Fleet to warp to the dark side of planet Kana where the spacecraft I'm transferring from First Fleet will join you. Shundite sensors won't detect your combined forces when they reappear in normal space because they'll be hidden by the planets' mass. You'll only have a few minutes to organize your battle formations and attack them from behind. Finally, I'm ordering you to assume full command of this mission. Act quickly Vice Admiral Maur, or the fight will be lost."

It was a battle for the history books. In the face of superior numbers, Admiral Kuza split his already outnumbered First Fleet and transferred it to Second Fleet, which came screaming out of concealment behind planet Kana and tore into the rear of the assembled Shundite forces. Commanders of the Shundite Alliance were taken completely by surprise.

Hundreds of Cydonian interceptors ripped through the Shundite formation from behind - blowing several dozen Alliance spacecraft out of the sky on their first pass through. Damaged and burning Shundite spacecraft littered the sky when the interceptors wheeled around for their second attack.

Vice Admiral Maur ordered assault ships Anvil, Axe, Drill, Charger, Knife and Spear to detach from Second Fleet, establish an attack squadron and begin a ground assault upon Kana. Completely unopposed by Shundite fighters that had sailed off to attack Kuza's fleet, the attack squadron began a general nuclear bombardment of the planet's surface. Troop landings followed almost immediately. As a result of the surface action, calls for help from planet Kana served only to add to the confusion already crippling the Shundite fleet commanders' appraisal of battle conditions. Their ability to respond to the rapidly changing situation collapsed.

From his perspective in the rear of the Shundite fleet, Vice Admiral Maur realized their hope for surprise had succeeded. He sent a QC message to Admiral Kuza advising him to reverse his feigned retreat from advancing Alliance spacecraft. In response to Maur's request First Fleet changed its tactics from a defensive posture to offensive action. First Fleet attacked the Shundite forces opposing it – catching Shundite spacecraft off balance in the middle of a pincer movement. First Fleet attacked the Shundite battle formation in front. Battlecruisers, heavy cruisers and interceptors from Second Fleet trashed it from behind.

Without a coordinated command structure to oppose them, Cydonian interceptors flew circles around between and within Shundite fighter formations. Alliance fighter squadrons were cut to pieces.

Confusion reigned among Shundite commanders. Nobody seemed to know where the attacks were coming from or how to form an appropriate response. Their spacecraft burst into flames and fell out of the sky like a holiday fireworks display. Death stalked the Shundite Alliance. Nothing they did seemed to work to their advantage. Their only successful maneuver proved to be an emergency warp withdrawal. Shundite spacecraft that weren't already crippled or destroyed moved toward their interspatial transfer point and began to disappear from normal space.

Realizing the Alliance was attempting to preserve what remained of its fleet, Vice Admiral Maur ordered his damaged flagship and Pathfinder-73 to prepare for a warp pursuit. Voice messages were exchanged with Fleet Admiral Kuza requesting permission to follow Shundite warp traces wherever they led.

"Admiral Kuza, this is Vice Admiral Maur. We need to arrange a pursuit of the enemy. They're disorganized and if we strike soon enough we can destroy what remains of their ability to make war against us."
"We don't know where they're going, Maur."
"Pathfinder-73 can follow the warp traces of the retreating Shundite spacecraft. My flagship, Sirenum, has suffered damage to its sensors, but our weapons are intact. Sirenum can escort Pathfinder-73 to insure its safe return. If we can learn the destination of the Shundite fleet we can use that knowledge to attack them wherever they've gone. We can make an end of the remnants of their fleet as well as any world they rely upon for support."
"The main body of the enemy fleet at Kana has been routed. Its' remnants are proving difficult to silence. We've still got a lot of scattered fighting going on, Maur. I'm not sure we can organize another attack so soon."
"It's my hope we can do so, Admiral. If we can't, then we'll at least know where to attack them as soon as we're able."
"Very well. You may follow the Shundite warp traces wherever they lead. Just make sure you get back to tell us where they went."
"Aye sir. We're on our way."

Hours later most of the remaining Shundite spacecraft in the V2500 star system had either surrendered or been destroyed. Cydonian spacecraft assumed defensive positions in the event of a Shundite counter-attack even though none was really expected. Search and rescue missions were begun to recover damaged spacecraft and wounded personnel. Morale was high, but many of the spacecraft crews remained edgy.

Fleet Admiral Kuza was in his quarters composing an after-battle report to the Pentagon when an emergency QC alert activated his private video console.

"There's been an unfortunate development," the Captain of Pathfinder-73 reported.

"Have you returned from following the Shundite fleet, Captain?"

"Yes Admiral. We have the coordinates of their planetary base. It's in the KIC 8462852 star system. That's Boyajian's Star about four hundred fifty parsecs from Cydonia. There's also been an accident."

"What's the nature of the accident, Captain?"

"We sustained some damage from patrolling Shundite fighters during our reconnaissance. Vice Admiral Maur's flagship Sirenum was heavily damaged when it attempted to protect us."

"Were both spacecraft able to make the return warp jump?"

"Yes Admiral, but our own patrol interceptors fired on us when we resolved into normal space above planet Kana. Sirenum was destroyed."

"WHAT! How did this happen, Captain?"

"Sirenum's communication system had been damaged by Shundite fighters during our recon. Operation of its automatic identification beacon was intermittent. I believe our interceptor patrol didn't realize they were firing on one of our own spacecraft."

"Were there any survivors?"

"No, Admiral. Our interceptors have been very efficient today."

"Very well. In the morning I want to see a full report on your mission including an account of Vice Admiral Maur's death."

Kuza switched off his console and considered how the loss of his best leader would impact the next phase of the Cydonian campaign against the Shundite Alliance. Attention would now focus on the KIC 8462852 star system, but now he'd have to reevaluate his command structure. Available commanders weren't as flexible or capable as Vice Admiral Maur had been.

Planet Kana surrendered the next day.

Out-gunned and out-numbered, the Cydonian Space Service had won an incredible victory against overwhelming odds at the Battle of Kana. Despite its success, Cydonian expansion had come to an end. Planet Kana would prove to be the last addition to the Cydonian Star Empire's list of vassal worlds. The price had been too high and resistance, despite the recent Shundite defeat, would continue to increase.

* * *

News of the Dedication Day assassination attempt upon the Leader's life shocked and angered the citizens of Cydonia. Those who suffered under the heel of its' cruelty on other worlds quietly rejoiced. When news of the victory at the Battle of Kana hit video screens and print media, Cydonian citizens were jubilant. On the home world everyone celebrated. The same story on vassal worlds slammed every one who heard it with disappointment, depressed anger and resentment.

Dark days of oppression continued to press down upon the lives of untold millions who hated Cydonia more than ever before. Cystapo officers all across the Empire demanded participation in flag waving parades. Vassal worlds would applaud the victory or suffer consequences if they didn't. Those that refused to comply were arrested – their assets seized, their homes plowed into the ground. All across the Cydonian Star Empire, mutiny sedition and rebellion sprang up like weeds in a summer garden.

* * *

Raene sat on her terrace overlooking the Tempe Terra plain below. Cydonia's largest hub of spacecraft and aircraft activity was always interesting to watch, but it wasn't the traffic that inspired her retreat to the terrace that day. Her heavy heart was laboring from the weight of recent family revelations.

"Mother I'm so excited about our victory at Kana," daughter Janian had declared.

"It's a great achievement," Raene admitted.

"I want to be a part of it."

"What?"

"I'm going to join Space Service and become an interceptor pilot. I want to fight our enemies."

"Janian, you know I've always been loyal to the Leader but I think you're convictions are a bit misplaced. Our government isn't altogether altruistic. It has deep problems and I think the military is one of them."

"What do you mean? Patriotism is needed now more than ever. They've tried to kill our Leader. They've raided our trade routes and loyal worlds everywhere. It's intolerable. Something needs to be done and I want to be part of the team that establishes peace among the stars."

"I'm not sure making war against those who disagree with us is the best way to do that," Raene said.

"What do you expect us to do? Shall we blow them kisses and send them flowers? No. I think the only thing the Shundite Alliance understands is a missile up their tail pipe."

"JANIAN. Such language isn't to be used in this house. Please calm down. I know you're excited about the victory news, but I don't believe this is a good time to enlist."

"Sorry mom," Janian said as she marched toward the door. "I just wanted to tell you I've already signed up. I'm leaving this afternoon to begin my training. I'd hoped you'd be happy about it. I'm a patriot, but now I'm wondering about your convictions."

"My dear, I've always supported the Leader. You know this to be true. I just think there are men around him that aren't acting in the best interests of our people or the Empire."

"Maybe they are and maybe they aren't," Janian declared. "As of today I'm one of them."

The door slammed behind the young woman - leaving her mother alone in the middle of the terrace. A breeze from the valley wafted faint cheers from celebrations and parades below as tears appeared in Raene's eyes.

Behind the open door to his bedroom, Raene's son Vladian had listened to the conversation between his mother and sister with concerned interest. He too had planned to enter Space Service, but didn't know how to break the news to his mother. After Janian's stormy announcement and angry retreat, Vladian decided he should do what he'd determined to do and not say anything about it. He'd just leave a letter on his bed and quietly avoid an argument. After all, it was his life to live wasn't it?

* * *

Half a year was a long time to prepare an assault against the Shundite at KIC 8462852. It was far too long considering Vice Admiral Maur's desire to chase the enemy immediately after its defeat at Kana. Pursuit of an enemy in retreat from a battlefield is something no military commander has the luxury to ignore, but Admiral Kuza would insist Cydonian forces were too damaged and scattered for a pursuit of the enemy. Maur wasn't around to argue otherwise.

During the fleets' rehabilitation, the Leader invited Admiral Kuza to the capital for an award presentation and discussion of his plans for the next action against the Shundite Alliance. In a private conference, the Leader asked Admiral Kuza for details of his plans.

"Repairs on our spacecraft are nearly complete as is the training of new crew replacements," Fleet Admiral Kuza reported.

"When and where do you plan to execute further action against the Shundite Alliance?"

"With your approval, I intend to attack the Shundite base at KIC 8462852 in less than two weeks."

"That soon? What of new spacecraft and new leaders? How do you propose to organize the fleet?"

"It takes a long time to build a modern spacecraft and install weapon systems. We can't do it quickly and I don't believe the Shundite can do so either. During the Battle of Kana we destroyed about half their fleet, making them equal in size to our own. Assuming Shundite capacity to repair and replace their spacecraft is no greater than ours, I expect the next engagement between us to be of equal numbers. We'll be evenly matched."

The Leader smiled at the Admiral's estimation of the situation, "I'm happy to hear that. If you could defeat a Shundite force twice your size I have no doubt you can destroy one equal to your own."

"Even better my Leader, I'm supremely confident our will to win is vastly superior to theirs. I believe our spacecraft and our crews can defeat anything the Shundite Alliance assembles against us. We are invincible."

Admiral Kuza's words pleased the Leader greatly. They were exactly what he wanted to hear, "Very well Admiral Kuza. How do you propose to organize your forces?"

"During the Battle of Kuza our spacecraft were organized into two fleets. This time I'll reorganize it into three fleets to allow for greater flexibility. I'll continue to command First Fleet. I've assigned Commodore Bira, who directed the assault force at Kana, to command Second Fleet."

"Who have you placed in command of Third Fleet?"

"With your permission I'd like to promote Provost Marshal Yaxkin of the Space Service Academy to the position of Third Fleet Commodore."

"Done," the Leader said. "Do you really believe two weeks will be sufficient time to complete preparations?"

"We've added quite a few vessels to the fleet by converting transport spacecraft. It's cheaper and quicker than building new ships from the drawing board. I think we'll be ready in time."

"Very well. I believe your preparations are adequate to the task at hand. May the solar winds be at your back and may your aim be true. Good hunting to you and your fleet."

Admiral Kuza was confident his fleet could defeat any force arrayed against him. He believed his victory at Kana, still fresh in everyone's mind, proved his crews could accomplish any task assigned to them. Unfortunately his attitude suffered from several points of critical weakness.

Kuza's decisions would be clouded by over-confidence and blinded by a lack of information about Shundite locations numbers and intentions. His crews, now mostly raw recruits, were eager but untested in the fire of battle. Every probe and pilotless drone that had been sent to KIC 8462852 had disappeared without so much as a single bit of data transmitted back to Cydonian listening posts. Kuza would be sailing into the dark, completely unaware of what awaited him.

As the Admiral strode out of the Pentagon Pyramid toward a waiting staff car he noticed a strangely clad man standing beneath a lamppost. As he passed the figure he politely acknowledged the man's presence and said good morning.

"Nothing good about it," the man said. "Nothing good for you and nothing good for the Empire. You will return to this place with a damaged career and a wrecked fleet."

Kuza heard the voice, but was too focused on the task ahead of him. His staff car arrived and he seated himself inside. As it pulled away from the curb he glanced back at the lamppost for a glimpse of the strange man. The figure was nowhere to be seen.

* * *

'I don't believe our fleet can score another easy victory,' columnist Galelian would write in an article submitted to his editor.

"I don't know if I can print this," his editor said. "People will accuse us of having a defeatist attitude."

"At the very least my story will be controversial. Our readership has dropped recently because there's been a glut of good news. I think people will respond to a different diet of material."

"Are you hoping for defeat, Galelian?"

"What I want or what the Empire wants is irrelevant. What we've chosen is at hand. Our readers deserve a clear understanding of the consequences of our collective actions.

I'm a veteran of Space Service and I know things don't always go as planned. There may be reverses in the upcoming battle. We should understand the risks and prepare accordingly."

"Very well. I'll approve your piece for publication, but I'm going to place it in the editorial section. Do the necessary rewrite for it to appear as an opinion piece. Tone it down a bit. I'm sure there'll be objections no matter how you phrase it. Chip away at your story. Make it less antagonistic toward the government.

I'll probably spend the rest of the week apologizing to every idiot who thinks they know how to run a media outlet. What I really don't want is a call from the Cystapo."

It didn't take long before intimations of disaster in the distant regions of space began to percolate into the awareness of the news media. An official press release from Space Service stated a large battle had been fought at KIC 8462852 between the Shundite Alliance and Admiral Kuza's fleet. That was it and that was all.

People in the news business realized Space Service was oddly quiet about the incident. Like many other media editors, Galelian's boss became suspicious when he began hearing unhappy rumors from private sources. In consideration of the unusual situation, Galelian wasn't surprised when he was called into the editorial office for a closed-door conference.

Before his editor uttered a word Galelian began by saying he thought something had gone terribly wrong at KIC 8462852.

"I know it for a fact," his editor answered. "Begin by telling me what you've learned."

"The campaign began with all sorts of bravado," Galelian said. "Now things are unusually quiet. There aren't any exclamations of victory coming out of Space Service. One would suppose a confrontation of that magnitude would result in something of a positive nature. They haven't said a thing. At the very least they should've released a casualty list."

"They released those lists after the Battle of Kana," the editor recalled.

"Yes, but nothing is being heard this time," Galelian said. "What fact has come to your attention?"

"I've learned two things," the editor said. "Actually they're more like qualified rumors. One is from a friend at Space Service Academy and the others come from healthcare professionals I used to work with when I was a reporter. Both sources suggest we lost the battle with the Shundite. Apparently we lost very badly."

"What sort of speculation are you talking about?"

"Following the battle Admiral Kuza was either ordered to return to the Pentagon or appeared before the Leader on his own volition. Either way, Kuza offered his resignation."

Galelian sat back in his chair and considered the news, "That's very significant."

"It's more than significant. We're dancing on the cusp of military disaster here. No Admiral has ever offered his resignation after a battle.

I think he was responsible for leading our fleet into a major defeat and wanted to do the honorable thing by resigning. I've also heard Commodore Yaxkin was killed and that Third Fleet under his command was torn to pieces - completely destroyed."

"Wasn't Yaxkin the former Provost Marshal of Space Service Academy?"

"Yes he was," the editor said.

"That's incredible news, boss. I've been a critic of the military for years, but I never thought it would come to this. What's the other rumor you've heard?"

"I'm acquainted with doctors nurses and hospital administrative types all over Cydonia. After I heard a story from a couple of them I made quiet inquires of my other acquaintances in the healthcare field. They all confirm the same situation."

The editor paused to sip a cup of tea. His hand shook visibly. Galelian waited for him to compose himself.

"A huge number of body bags have been shipped into receiving areas at the old Hesperia spaceport. They arrive on military transport ships in the middle of the night and are off-loaded under guard as though the dead were confidential material. It's as though the military is ashamed of the number of fatalities and doesn't want anyone to know how many have been counted."

"Have you heard anything else?"

"Yes. Military and civilian hospitals have received a large number of patients with battle related wounds and injuries."

"What sort of injuries?"

"Burns mostly – radiation burns. A lot of them have broken bones and severed limbs. Many have been impaled with bits of shrapnel in various parts of their bodies. They're admitted in the middle of the night as patients. Hospitals and trauma centers have been forbidden to notify relatives. The military has told them they'd take care of it, but as far as I know no notification has been forthcoming from anybody."

"Do you want me to cover this story," Galelian asked.

"Yes, but do it quietly. We don't want the Cystapo getting aroused by too many questions asked of the wrong people. When you write something up, I want to see it first. Don't send it to your department head."

Galelian passed his hand through his hair, "I have no idea where to start with this. It's way too big."

"Start with the lack of notifications of family members. They deserve to hear of the death and wounding of their kin," the editor said. "That should be the easiest rabbit trail to follow and one that won't necessarily raise the ire of the Cystapo. Start with that – then investigate reasons or stories of what went wrong. Explore that sad story very carefully."

"Sounds good to me," Galelian said. "Our families deserve to know what happened."

"I'm going to assign another journalist to work with you," the editor said. "Her name is Isi and she's as interested in these murky matters as you are. You can trust her. Be careful, Galelian. The Cystapo is watching everything we say and do."

"I understand," Galelian said. "If what we're hearing is true, the Empire has suffered a major military defeat. Recovery from this situation may be difficult. If this defeat is as bad as it seems to be, the future will be pretty bleak."

Galelian had no idea how bad things were going to become. Nobody did.

* * *

Cydonia never recovered from the defeat at KIC 8462852. The high water mark of their attempts to conquer planets beyond their own ended four hundred fifty parsecs from the home world. From that point on, the retreat and collapse of the Cydonian Star Empire gained speed and devastating intensity.

No one on Cydonia imagined how the war would end except for a strangely clad figure that appeared here and there on the home world preaching a message of death and destruction. Glad times faded into memory. The shriveling Empire began to suffer shortages and rationing.

Chapter 9
KUZA'S LAST STAND

Raene stepped onto her terrace and shivered from the cold morning air. Clutching a cup of steaming herbal tea in both hands she gently lifted the beverage to her lips and sipped – hoping the hot liquid would warm her insides. The sky was still black three hours before sunrise in the east, but above the opposite horizon the Phobos moon had already made its appearance - as though it too was eager to witness the beginning of a new day.

Sleep always eluded Raene when a member of her family was about to depart on a long assignment. It was still dark when she gave up trying. Dropping into a comfortable padded lounger, she waited and watched for the scheduled launch of her daughters' transport. If all preparations went as planned Janian would go up at sunrise.

Tempe Terra was the cartographers name for a vast plain that stretched out miles to the west of Raene's home. It was from there the military and the merchants launched their craft into space. Although the spaceport was miles away on the eastern slopes of the Tharsis Mountains, she could sometimes see its activity from her terrace on the Sacra Mensa ridge. The view was a tonic that never disappointed.

Despite the early morning hour hundreds of vehicles were already moving along the network of highways under her gaze - illuminating the plain with pinpoints of artificial light. Raene shivered and sipped her tea. It was cooling off already and she'd only been out in the air a few minutes. She searched for a nearby blanket to throw over her legs and in so doing she almost missed the launch and interspatial transit.

Sleep caught up with her like a gentle thief, aided and abetted by the chill night air as it mingled with the warmth of her padded blanket. She spent many nights out on the terrace when sleep was a stranger. Time passed unaware until a glint of sunshine teased her eyes awake. The realization that Phobos was beyond its zenith and that three hours had passed forced her into crisp awareness. She stood to her feet just in time to witness the launch of several vessels in Janian's group.

Beams of sunlight colored the ground as pinpoints of white light appeared out on the spaceport planitia. Raene didn't know which one carried her daughter, but it didn't really matter. Several launched at once, leaping into the air at blinding speed only to join other points of white light all swinging around the sky in a lazy circle. One by one each of the lights winked out of the space they occupied in the upper atmosphere. Somewhere beyond the familiar stars of home the transport that carried Janian returned to normal space. One of the newest pilots in the Space Service would arrive at her destination before her mother could return to the comfort of her lounger. Out on Tempe Terra a new day's commotion had begun.

Raene wondered if there really was a point to all the activity, a reason for all the dedication to duty, and an ultimate purpose for all the personal sacrifice they'd been asked to make for the endless years of war they'd suffered. Such thoughts were seditious and Raene knew it. She comforted herself with mind numbing political slogans until she nodded off to sleep once again.

* * *

"I'd like to begin this interview by thanking you for providing a testimony of the recent battle for our readers," Galelian said. "For purposes of anonymity everyone should understand we're going to call you Lieutenant Commander Black. Obviously that's not your real name or rank is it?"

"No, it isn't," Lt. Commander Black replied. "I appreciate this opportunity to tell what really happened at KIC 8462852."

"That's not the popular name used by members of the fleet is it," Isi asked.

"No, we used to call it the WTF star because of its odd astronomical characteristics."

Isi asked what the odd perturbations of the WTF star meant. Did they indicate the presence of a super-civilization?

"We weren't there in the capacity of explorers. We were there to fight the Shundite Alliance. We never determined to any degree of satisfaction what the star's emanations meant."

"When we first spoke to you it was our understanding you were stationed aboard [censored] for the Battle of Kana as well as the Battle of WTF," Isi said.

Black chuckled a bit, "That's a strange way to refer to the fight, but yes I was the [censored] officer on both occasions."

"Can you tell us what Admiral Kuza's original battle plan hoped to accomplish?"

"To the best of my knowledge Admiral Kuza intended to repeat the fleet movements that were so successful at the Battle of Kana. He divided the fleet into separate groups or sub-fleets. When First Fleet dropped out of warp at its designated interspatial transit point, Kuza directed Second and Third Fleets to the opposite sides of the Shundite forces arrayed against it."

"Is that the way the battle began," Isi asked.

"Yes, for a little while. When First Fleet dropped out of warp the Alliance fleet assumed an unusual formation. Their spacecraft arranged themselves in the shape of a convex lens or parabolic dish."

"Do you mean the formation was curved," Isi asked.

"Yes. It was curved away from First Fleet's position in space, sort of bent behind itself – the edges being further away from First Fleet than the front of the formation."

"How did Admiral Kuza react to that discovery?"

"He didn't change the battle plan. In retrospect he should have. As planned he ordered Second and Third fleet to drop out of warp behind the Shundite formation. That was a big mistake."

"Why?"

"Because the parabolic formation focused more fire upon its rear areas than the front. Third Fleet was cut to pieces in minutes. Second Fleet barely had time to react before their spacecraft began to be incinerated by concentrations of Shundite fire power."

"What was First Fleet doing all this time?"

"According to plan, First Fleet attacked the Shundite formation front and center, which was its weakest point, but Alliance defensive counter-fire was nearly as effective as First Fleet's attack. Their numbers were less in front, but so were those of First Fleet.

The majority of our spacecraft were concentrated in Second and Third Fleet. When Third Fleet ceased to exist as an effective fighting force, Second Fleet began to receive the major concentration of Shundite fire. Most of Second Fleet's crews were green – untested under the conditions of battle stress. Their reaction time was poor and weapon accuracy minimal at best. We believe they suffered heavy losses without damaging Alliance spacecraft to any significant degree.

Second Fleet was hemorrhaging spacecraft at an alarming rate when Commodore Bira requested permission from Admiral Kuza for an emergency withdrawal. By the time Bira received permission to retreat, Second Fleet had lost more than half its number. The battle ended when First Fleet, the first and last group on the battlefield, warped away from the WTF star system with minimal damage."

Everyone was silent for a time. Lt. Commander Black's revelation of what had happened to the mighty Cydonian fleet was sobering news.

"How severely has the fleet been damaged, Commander?"

"I'd estimate the number of combat ready spacecraft is about twenty-five to thirty percent of its former strength. Seventy-five percent of our ships and crew were lost or damaged in the engagement. Some can be repaired, but even with those units brought back into service we can only hope for forty percent parity of our former strength."

"How much damage did we inflict upon the Shundite Alliance?"

"It's difficult to guess, but I think it's safe to assume their losses were negligible. We began the battle equally matched. At this point in time I'd estimate their effective over-all strength is four or five times that of our own."

* * *

Vladian awoke a few hours before dawn and quietly prepared to leave home. His recruiter had told him a vehicle would be waiting for him in the morning and that he wouldn't need to pack anything for the trip. Space Service would give him everything he needed.

Passing through the house for the last time, Vladian noticed his mother asleep in a heated lounge chair out on the terrace. It was freezing outside, yet she seemed to spend more time out there than in her bed. Dad was away on another construction job for the government and she slept alone as usual. Vladian made sure the front door was locked as he quietly closed it behind him.

Raene was going to cry when she read his letter. She was always crying about something. Uncle Modion used to say that when they were kids Raene would sneak off to funerals of people she didn't know just so she could cry about it. Modion said she could cry enough tears to cause Valles Marineris to go into flood stage and overflow its banks. She cried for days when Janian left for interceptor training. Vladian knew she'd cry again when she read his letter about entering Communications School.

As promised, the recruiter's vehicle was waiting for him when he reached the street. Tiny flakes of gently falling snow glittered in the glare of the streetlight. He entered the vehicle and looked back for a moment as they motored away. Vladian didn't realize it at the time, but he'd remember that morning, remember leaving home, for the rest of his long lonely life.

* * *

Admiral Kuza left his staff car and walked slowly toward the Pentagon Pyramid building. He grimaced from pain in his stomach. It was nerves, he told himself. It had started after the Battle of KIC 8462852 and gotten worse when he returned to Cydonia. Not wanting any distractions from the meeting, Kuza swallowed a medication to take the edge off his pain.

The Leader had insisted on this meeting, but Kuza was less than enthusiastic about its prospects. He knew or suspected another operation would be required of the fleet, but any action other than repelling the increasing number of raids and planetary skirmishes was problematic. The fleet was out numbered and out gunned to the degree that seeking any sort of contest with the Shundite Alliance was virtual suicide.

He walked past the lamppost where a strange figure had once stood - predicting disaster for him and the fleet. Nobody was there this time, which was a relief. Admiral Kuza didn't need to hear dire predictions today. Meeting with the Leader would be bad enough.

When Kuza was ushered into the Leader's office his worst fears were realized. The Great Man was pacing back and forth across the carpeted room muttering something in whispers. Seated in a chair in front of the Leaders' desk was Commodore Bira – looking like a schoolboy who'd been lectured by his teacher for some infraction of the rules.

Admiral Kuza exchanged glances with Bira and realized he was a dead man. Whatever words came out of the Leader's mouth, whatever decision he'd arrived at, would result in his demise. He decided to put his personal matters in order as soon as the meeting ended.

The Leader spoke as though he was lecturing ignorant children, "We've arrived at a crisis, gentlemen. As you are no doubt aware, our fleet has been reduced to about half its previous size."

Kuza reminded himself it was more like thirty percent, but he wasn't going to argue with a man who could have him taken out and shot for insubordination.

"As a result of your recent defeat, the size of our Empire and its influence upon remote star systems has shriveled to a fraction of its former size. Shundite inspired secession, mutiny, skirmishes, raids and sabotage has crippled interstellar trade routes and inspired withdrawal from centuries old trade agreements.

The economic drain on our Empire has reached critical levels. We can't sustain our military-industrial capacity to resist the Shundite Alliance much longer. A protracted defensive posture is out of the question. We must carry the fight to them, gentlemen. We must win a decisive victory."

Kuza couldn't hold his tongue, "My Leader, we are endeavoring to resist these raids even as we speak. It's difficult because of the reduced capacity of our fleet. Our interceptor squadrons are performing a heroic job despite not having enough experienced pilots or adequate repair facilities. We're endeavoring to rebuild the fleet, but such an effort takes time to accomplish. The Shundite fleet is simply too large for us to engage with any hope of success."

The Leader slammed his fist on a nearby table and screamed, "TIME is a luxury we do not have, Admiral. I didn't call this meeting to hear EXCUSES. Your job is to defeat the Shundite Alliance. We will NOT surrender another world another asteroid or another speck of space dust to them. Therefore I have no choice but to order you to assemble all available fleet assets and attack them at Wolf 359."

"Wolf 359," Commodore Bira asked. "Why Wolf 359?"

"The Wolf 359 system is two point six parsecs from this room, Commodore. That's how close the Shundite fleet will approach Cydonia in the coming days. The Cystapo has learned a small Alliance task force will attempt to make a landing on the fifth planet quite soon. You are to meet them and destroy as many of their spacecraft as practicable."

Admiral Kuza knew his opinion wouldn't be accepted, but had to give it anyway, "With all due respect My Leader our fleet cannot engage the Shundite Alliance. They are simply too numerous for us to defeat."

"I'm not ordering you to defeat their entire fleet, Admiral. Our intelligence suggests only a portion of it will attack Wolf 359. The Alliance believes we are too weak and crippled to mount any sort of opposition. As a consequence, they'll deploy reduced numbers for their invasion. We estimate sufficient resources are on hand for us to defeat them. You CAN and you MUST block their planned advance. It's vitally important to our overall war effort. We need time to implement a technological breakthrough."

The Leader paused and muttered, "I have something in mind."

"What sort of technology are you referring to My Leader," Commodore Bira asked. When The Leader didn't respond he repeated his question.

"I apologize if my concentration wandered for a moment. I have other issues on my mind today," The Leader said. "What I'm about to tell you is top secret compartmentalized information. It does not leave this room and you are not to discuss it with anyone at any time. Is this understood?"

Admiral Kuza and Commodore Bira both nodded in agreement.

"Our research and development teams have successfully tested two new weapon systems. Both are nearly ready for operation in combat. Taken separately either of them can change the fortunes of war forever. One of them can vaporize an entire enemy fleet many parsecs away without launching a single spacecraft."

The Leader paused in the middle of his lecture. Both military men waited for him to continue, but only heard soft murmuring.

"I have something in mind," the Leader said quietly.

Admiral Kuza dared to interrupt, "If this is true sir, then we need only delay and defend against Shundite raids and fleet movements. We don't need to seek an encounter that would jeopardize our fleet assets."

"Do you not appreciate the significance of star charts, Admiral? Do you not understand there are only a few remaining outposts and vassal worlds between Wolf 359 and Cydonia? The enemy is literally at our gates. We need to stop them now before their spacecraft appear in the sky above us. Your orders are to assemble the fleet and engage the enemy without delay. The time for discussion and debate is over. My decision is final."

Admiral Kuza and Commodore Bira stood to attention and saluted the Leader.

"Any questions gentlemen?"

"None, sir."

"Good hunting to you both. We'll be watching with great interest."

Kuza and Bira left the Leaders' office, but as the door closed behind them they thought they heard his voice as it whispered something.

Both men walked together down the long corridors and elevators of the Pentagon building to Admiral Kuza's office. When they arrived and could speak privately Kuza told the Commodore he was going to recommend Bira's promotion to the rank of Rear Admiral.

"Thank you sir," Bira said.

"I'm going to organize our spacecraft into two fleets this time. I'll command First Fleet and you'll command Second Fleet. There won't be any fancy formations or attack tactics. We go straight in hit the Shundite invasion force and get out as quickly as possible. Consider this a raid in force. Hopefully we'll survive."

"Agreed, sir."

"If something happens to me I want you to assume full command of the entire fleet and warp them out of the area."

"Where should we go, sir?"

"Wherever you can find a dark place to hide and lick your wounds."

* * *

First Fleet resolved into normal space near the fifth planet of the Wolf 359 star system. When he examined his long-range sensor data Admiral Kuza discovered the Shundite invasion force had already begun a bombardment of the planet's surface, but there was something odd about their methods. Finding no evidence of any other Alliance formations in the area he sent a QC message to Rear Admiral Bira approving Second Fleet's arrival as originally planned. Second Fleet appeared soon after receiving Kuza's order.

In a QC voice communication to Admiral Kuza, Bira advised his superior officer that caution should be taken prior to attacking the Shundite forces.

"Why are you hesitating," Admiral Kuza asked. "Assume attack formation. We're going to strike the Shundite formation front and center as we should have at KIC 8462852."

"Examine your sensors, Admiral. They've been using standard high explosive charges to bombard the planet. Most of those have landed in unpopulated areas. They haven't used nuclear weapons as is our standard practice. They're also altering their formation for defense."

"We're going in, Bira. Changes in their formation are evidence they've detected our arrival. We won't surprise them, but as we are in a position of superior numbers. I don't see that as a problem. There's no reason for caution at this point in time. The force we're looking at is a third the size of our own. If we strike them hard and fast we can bag the whole crowd.

No more debate Rear Admiral. Position Second Fleet on the starboard side of First Fleet. As soon as your spacecraft are ready we'll move."

FROM: FLEET 1
WOLF 359 STAR SYSTEM OPERATIONS
BATTLECRUISER OLYMPUS MONS 030521ADSK
ADMIRAL SIDRON KUZA, COMMANDING

TO: CYDONIA MILITARY COMMAND
SPACE SERVICE HEADQUARTERS

ACTION BULLETIN

ARRIVAL WOLF 359 PLANET 5 WITH FIRST AND SECOND FLEET. NO UNUSUAL INCIDENTS OR OBSERVATIONS DURING TRANSIT.

SHUNDITE INVASION FORCE APPEARS TO BE BOMBARDING PLANET 5 WITH HIGH EXPLOSIVE CHARGES. NO GROUND ASSAULT AS OF THIS TRANSMISSION.

WE ARE PREPARING TO INDERDICT THE SHUNDITE INVASION.

THIS IS A BATTLE ALERT.

-30-

QC TRANSCRIPTION WOLF 359 ### MLB7221-1

The Cydonian combined fleet drove into the center of the Shundite defense formation with all weapons firing. Initial contact with forward elements of the Alliance was encouraging, but not as destructive as Admiral Kuza had hoped. The Shundite Alliance invasion group had assumed an unorthodox defensive configuration.

The Shundite defensive position Rear Admiral Bira had expressed concern about was in the form of a three-dimensional checkerboard or cube. Instead of forming a firing line with all units in a row or wall, the Shundite spacecraft divided into rows and columns. A few lightly armed spacecraft created a box defense like a small fort or firebase. Open spaces separated each small fortress box from its neighbor's defensive box, allowing the separate boxes to support their neighbor front and back as well as left and right top and bottom. The formation allowed greater latitude in its field of fire than a standard firing line. Any attacker would be subject to a crossfire defense regardless of its direction of attack or position in space.

A checkerboard cube permitted defense in depth. Row upon row in alternating positions prevented any sudden enemy breakthrough and insured cohesion of the entire group should such an eventuality occur. The Cydonian combined fleet drove deep into the Shundite checkerboard cube – penetrating several rows and layers of box forts.

"Admiral Kuza to Second Fleet – we estimate the rear perimeter of the Shundite defense will be breached in a few moments. Our losses at this point are approximately ten percent. We're in good shape. Report your situation."

"Rear Admiral Bira to First Fleet – our losses are approximately eight percent. How do you wish to follow up on the breakthrough?"

"When we achieve a breakthrough you'll swing Second Fleet ninety degrees to the right and attack the Shundite group on your starboard side. First Fleet will attack to port. We'll form a wedge in the middle of the Shundite formation and separate it into two groups. If the group in front of you is too strong I'll come to your aid. If the group in front of us is too strong you will assist us."

Results of the action against the Shundite invasion group were encouraging. As Admiral Kuza and Rear Admiral Bira's fleets attacked left and right the Shundite checkerboard fractured, but didn't shatter. They separated slowly – retreating from the Cydonian attacks.

Kuza and Bira found themselves fighting against two smaller Shundite checkerboard cubes instead of only a single large one. Instead of weakening, each separate box fort retained its strength and command cohesion. The Cydonian attack was succeeding, but taking much longer than Kuza's original estimate. The Shundite defense was trading space for time.

"Rear Admiral Bira to First Fleet – our situation is superior. Enemy forces in front of us appear to have been reduced to about forty percent of their original number. I believe we've accomplished our purpose to demonstrate in force. I also believe the Shundite's purpose here is to delay us for some reason. This situation isn't about preventing an invasion of planet five. It's about something else. We're stuck in this like flies on flypaper."

"Get a grip on yourself," Admiral Kuza responded angrily. "You sound like you're about to crap your pants. We're winning and we're going to keep winning until we've won it all."

"Please consider the big picture Admiral Kuza. It might be wise to withdraw while we're in a position of strength and relatively undamaged. I'm not comfortable with this situation - not comfortable at all. It's been too easy. I believe you should order a withdrawal."

Kuza's blood was up. Complete victory was in his grasp and vindication for his recent defeat nearly at hand. His stomach pain had miraculously disappeared.

Kuza refused to consider Rear Admiral Bira's advice, "Withdraw? In our hour of triumph? I think you overestimate their chances. You are to continue Second Fleet's attack. We will attack until there is no enemy left to resist us. The Shundite Alliance will discover this day that Cydonia remains a powerful and dangerous enemy. We will not yield an inch of the Cydonian Star Empire to the Shundite Alliance."

To Rear Admiral Bira it seemed only moments passed after receiving Admiral Kuza's message. In actuality several minutes had ticked off the clock when the entire Shundite Fleet appeared in full force. Appearing suddenly in normal space, its spacecraft assumed positions above below behind and in front of the battle zone between the Cydonian Fleet and the checkerboard cube formation – effectively encapsulating Admiral Kuza's entire force. It was First and Second Fleet that had been bagged, not the Shundite Alliance.

Shundite attacks initially focused upon Admiral Kuza's flagship, the proud Battlecruiser Olympus Mons. Slightly more than five miles in length, she was the largest spacecraft to ever navigate the stars. Her firepower was equal to a fleet of smaller ships and her hanger bays were large enough to accommodate several interceptor squadrons as well as an assault ship. She was capable of invading an entire planet without any other spacecraft to support her.

A volley of Shundite high-energy weapons and missiles tore into her superstructure. One missile scored a direct hit on the battle bridge killing nearly everyone stationed there and blowing everyone else into the vacuum of space. A nuclear tipped self-guiding drone smashed into her amidships and detonated – destroying a full third of her length and rendering her into two separate defenseless parts. Admiral Kuza never knew what killed him.

FROM: FLEET 2
WOLF 359 STAR SYSTEM OPERATIONS
BATTLECRUISER ELYSIUM MONS 030521RAAB
REAR ADMIRAL AMARU BIRA, COMMANDING

TO: CYDONIA MILITARY COMMAND
SPACE SERVICE HEADQUARTERS

EMERGENCY BATTLE NOTIFICATION ALERT

SURPRISE ATTACK BY ENTIRE SHUNDITE ALLIANCE FLEET HAS US BOXED IN AND SURROUNDED. WE ARE UNDER VIGOROUS ATTACK. CANNOT WITHDRAW.

BATTLECRUISER OLYMPUS MONS DESTROYED. ADMIRAL KUZA KILLED IN ACTION. COMMAND OF ALL UNITS TRANSFERRED TO REAR ADMIRAL BIRA.

SECOND FLEET FLAGSHIP BATTLECRUISER ELYSIUM MONS HEAVILY DAMAGED.
HEAVY CRUISERS CIMMERIA AND TEMPE DESTROYED. NOACHIS DAMAGED.
LIGHT CRUISERS SIRENUM DESTROYED. NILI & CLARITAS SEVERALY DAMAGED.
FRIGATES LACUS AERIA AND OPHIR DESTROYED. LACUS & THARSIS DAMAGED.
ALL CUTTERS DESTROYED. PATHFINDER-21 DESTROYED.
PATHFINDER-20 ORDERED TO WITHDRAW WITH LOGS & RECORDS.

ADMIRAL TALAKO OF THE SHUNDITE ALLIANCE HAS DEMANDED SURRENDER.

TO PREVENT FURTHER EFFUSION OF BLOOD I AM TENDERING OUR SURRENDER
TO ADMIRAL TALAKO – EFFECTIVE IMMEDIATELY.

THIS IS OUR FINAL MESSAGE.

-30-

QC TRANSCRIPTION WOLF 359-1 ### WJ7221-1
* * *

When a spacecraft is destroyed in battle the place where it dies disappears. Solar wind and gravity wells disturb the debris field. If rescuers or survey teams arrive nothing is found at all. Evidence of a struggle or accident is swallowed up in the limitless expanse of empty space. Nothing remains of what was once an organized active wedding of humanity and machinery.

The dead disappear. No corpses remain and there are rarely any living survivors for rescue teams to carry away. There are no body parts to be collected bagged or buried. In space there isn't any place at all to anchor a memorial flagpole or headstone.

The once mighty Cydonian Fleet died in space near the fifth planet of the Wolf 359 star system. Only the victors and those who surrendered continued to live beyond the day of battle and only the Shundite Alliance knew where they went.

Chapter 10
POLITICS and RELIGION

Like a scorpion that stings itself to death when surrounded by fire, the Cydonian government, challenged by a war it could no longer win, began to commit organizational suicide. It began to kill its own people. No one saw it coming. No one was immune. No one could stop it.

News of the fleet's defeat at Wolf 359 was not well received in the cavernous galleries below the Pentagon Pyramid. A particularly vile rumor suggested the Leader, insane with anger and frustration, had personally shot a messenger as he delivered the bad news. Shocked and surprised at his wounds, the poor lad staggered a few steps and fell to the floor gasping for breath as blood and life gushed out of him. The Leader screamed obscenities at the young man and proceeded to march up and down the corridors muttering incomprehensibly - firing his gun at anything he chose. People who saw or heard him coming instinctively hid from sight. Broom closets became small sanctuaries, packed with people seeking refuge. Elevators, filled to capacity, evacuated hundreds of the Pentagon's occupants.

Cystapo squads arrested nearly every military and intelligence leader in the high command. Few above the rank of Captain survived the purge. Nobody knew what happened to those who were detained, but fresh bloodstains on many levels of the Pentagon suggested no good end.

One Cystapo squad broke into the home of a prominent military leader and encountered journalist Isi in the process of an interview. The government news service later announced everyone in the house had died as the result of a tragic fire.

* * *

The first Dedication Day was held during the administration of the Third World Leader, when air travel had become a normal part of life and space flight was still experimental. To foster unity and inspire a common goal, the Cydonian people were called to dedicate themselves to the construction of three large representations of the first Leader.

The first construction was a two-dimensional trial effort, a type of relief concept combining features of two-dimensional art with three-dimensional sculpture. The work was widely applauded and encouraged a second larger version that was completely three-dimensional. It too was a resounding success in that it inspired patriotic support of the government, which of course was its ultimate purpose. As a consequence of its acceptance and as one of the final acts of his life, the third world Leader commissioned the greatest effort of all — construction of an immense sculpture of the first Leader that would endure for all the years of future time.

It was carved out of a mountain of solid rock nearly a mile and a half wide and a bit more than four miles long. Its features were identical to its two predecessors in that it wore a warrior's helmet and faced the sky with an expression of grim determination. It would be large enough to be seen from space and would convey the resolute attitude of a soldier who had dedicated himself to the protection of his world from the terrors of the heavens.

In time, the actual name of the First Great Leader would fade from popular use, possibly because everyone realized the facial features of the third sculpture more closely resembled the third Leader than the first. Caution in avoidance of arrest for criticizing the third Leader's grandiose expression of conceit resulted in the adoption of a generic popular name for the edifice. It came to be simply called The Face.

Each year the anniversary of its completion was celebrated as a world holiday replete with mass rallies, parades, televised specials and home dinner parties. Nobody really cared about patriotic celebrations as much as they relished a day off from work. The Face may have been carved out of solid rock, but it's meaning had become hollow and thin.

* * *

On this Dedication Day Raene planned to open her home to friends and relatives for a private evening dinner party. Life had become difficult and bleak recently - different from years past. Everything had become scarce or too expensive. Food was rationed and even the amount of time one was allowed to watch video at home was restricted. Electrical service was spotty, not that Raene noticed much.

Summer and winter usually found her sleeping out on the terrace. The sounds of life and activity riding on the breeze from the valley below helped her feel less lonely. Everyone had left her. Rodion had gone off to work on a construction project in the east. Janian and Vladian were out in space or headed in that direction. Raene hoped the holiday would provide a grand excuse to invite guests and life back into her home if only for a short time. Perhaps the company would salve the emptiness in her heart.

Shortages and bad news had put everyone on edge, or dulled their minds to the unpleasant reality of routine living gone sour. Dedication Day was a welcome distraction. For one day at least things could resemble better days of the past. Raene saved her food and video ration to provide for her guests. Busy with her preparations, Raene even dared to hope for a call or letter from her absent family – until a man appeared at her door with unpleasant news.

Some guests arrived early. Others came late. Everyone was in a good mood, or at least tried to be. Raene greeted each of her guests with a valiant smile and gentle hug as they came through her door. Her bountiful table was heaped high with treats she'd made or others had brought with them. Food was the fuel for empty laughter and pointless chatter.

In the midst of fear so thick it was almost palpable and despite a desperate effort to ignore heavy clouds of depression and despair people everywhere congregated in a vain attempt to deny the inevitable future. The focal point of the party was to be the viewing of a televised speech by the Leader. Everyone hoped to hear goods news, but none expected it.

"What's Galelian doing here," one of the guests whispered to her companion. "Who invited him to the party?"

"He's an in-law I think."

"He's more like an outlaw. Every member of Raene's family is in service to the Leader. Her son Vladian recently received orders to report to Phobos station and her husband Rodion is Master Supervisor of subterranean improvements in the east. Her daughter has been on duty as an interceptor pilot in our Space Service for almost five years. Why can't Galelian be more like them?"

"He seems to have persuaded himself that he's being a patriot in his own way."

"Well it isn't my way and that's a fact."

Galelian stuffed a morsel of spicy food into his mouth and washed it down with a chilled beverage. He overheard a nearby couple talking about the upcoming speech and decided to insinuate himself into their conversation, "Hello. I don't believe we've met. I'm Galelian."

The couple introduced themselves and wondered what the Leader's speech would be about.

"I'm an investigative journalist by trade," Galelian said. "A lot of hints have reached my ears that suggest the annual speech will be more important than usual."

"What do you think the Leader is going to say? We love to hear his inspiring speeches. We have a collection of them, you know."

Galelian frowned in disagreement, "There've been quiet rumors circulating for days that this year's speech will be a watershed statement of significant importance to the entire planet. You'll definitely want to add this one to your library."

"What do you mean?"

"There are rumors the battles in space haven't gone well. I expect him to say something about it."

"That's a defeatist attitude. You need to be more supportive of our men and women in arms."

"I AM supportive of them," Galelian insisted. "My concern is for loss of life for no good reason. My concern is for the truth of things, not political gibberish that's repeated like slogans of a false religion. The war is going badly for us despite what we've been told. I dread what might be revealed today and what new demands may be made of us. Our future teeters on a razor's edge. Anyone with an ounce of intelligent consideration knows it."

Conversations were interrupted when someone switched on the video screen. The image of The Face as seen from orbit swam into view with the military crest of the Leader prominently displayed in the lower corner. Martial music played in the background before during and after the address, but it wasn't the Leader that appeared on screen. His presence was significantly absent as well as the location where it was usually delivered.

The traditional Dedication Day speech had always been presented outside, in the shadow of The Face. This time the speaker's podium had been placed in the Cydonian Sports Palace – a place where athletic competition and tournaments were held year round. The crowd in front of the podium was composed of government dignitaries and corporate supporters of the Leader and his programs – not average citizens, as had been the case previously. At exactly the appointed hour and minute a man ascended to the podium. Raene's guests all hushed as they waited to hear the words that would affect the lives of everyone on Cydonia.

* * *

"I am Defense Minister Rezon and I've been asked to address all Cydonia on this auspicious occasion."

Perhaps the rumors were true, Galelian thought. He'd heard the Leader had suffered some sort of psychotic break and that he'd been put under sedation, but he'd attributed that sort of talk to the lunatic fringe. Yet here it was – evidence the Leader was physically unable to carry out his duties. How badly had the fleet been defeated?

Galelian's attention returned to the video screen. Rezon was still speaking, *"In times long past, when our forebears struggled against drought and flood, there was born among us a confidence in ourselves. We learned that by working together we could solve any problem, work any miracle, reach any height, build any future and realize any hope. In fulfillment of that confidence, our first Leader, through tireless and selfless effort, united our separate tribes and distant cities into a single union, into one people and into a complete world altogether triumphant over those forces of nature that never failed never slackened and never sympathized with our need to live and build and dream. From generation to generation and with a continuing confidence in our ability to overcome any difficulty, we built within and upon this world the magnificent civilization we enjoy today.*

But there remained a great and terrible danger to overcome."

Here it comes, Galelian thought. History lessons and reminders of our heritage have been repeated every year. Have we now reached the end of it all? Will Rezon admit it?

"Despite our greatest achievements and despite our most heroic efforts a persistent constant threat has hung over our heads. As you are aware, our outposts our spacecraft and our trade routes in space have been continually and constantly attacked. An attempt upon our Leader's life has been made.

Despite our selfless efforts to establish good relations on every world and among every civilization there was one that refused the ways of peace. Every overture for harmony with them has been rejected, every encounter has been met with hostility, and every dutiful attempt to defend our property and our people has ended in open conflict.

I have been told and must now inform you that our fleet has suffered misfortunes and reversals during several battles in space. We can no longer hope to establish peace with our enemy. It is therefore my sad duty to inform you that as of sunrise today we have been officially at war with the Shundite Alliance.

We must remember that the military alone is in a position to defend us our homes and our families. If not for our selfless men and women in arms Cydonia would certainly fall under the influence of the Shundite Alliance. Shall we support them with our every effort and with one voice?"

The entire crowd in the Sports Palace erupted with cheers applause and explosive declarations of support for the military. Everyone in Raene's home joined with the televised applause.

Galelian couldn't remember a single attempt to establish peace with the Shundite Alliance. Had Rezon spoken another government lie? He'd have to check his files later.

"We must remember the Space Service and citizens of Cydonia alone have the ability to save civilization from the predations of this enemy and of all that is good and true and worthy of our allegiance. Shall we endeavor to give our support to the Leader and our military to finish the work so nobly begun?"

A standing ovation and cheers from the televised crowd lasted tens of minutes. No one in Raene's house remained seated. Everyone cheered and clapped and applauded until their hands hurt from the effort and their throats became raw from yelling. A semblance of quiet gradually returned to the Sports Palace, Raene's home and every other venue on the planet where people congregated in front of a video screen.

Rezon continued with his speech, *"The hammer blows of the Shundite Alliance have struck down the brave members of our fleet and now threaten to curse and to destroy that which we have built.*

Despite the hardship of space travel, despite the opposition of those we encountered among the stars, despite its cost in fortune and blood we have resolutely stood upon the unchanging confidence that has always been the hallmark of our character. We have always been constant in our determination to win the day. We are a people who are unyielding and confident in the ultimate victory of our cause, of our world and of our Leader.

Danger is now at hand and every Cydonian must act quickly and decisively to conquer as conquer we must. Do you believe with the Leader and us in the total final victory of the Cydonian people?"

Cheers and screams of support literally rolled out of the Sports Palace through the video screens and echoed in every home and public place. The turmoil in Raene's home was deafening as it must have been everywhere. Galelian found a paper napkin and stuffed pieces of it into his ears.

"Are you and the Cydonian people willing to work if the Leader asks ten twelve or even fourteen hours of work a day and to give everything for victory?"

Resounding screams of YES carried on the video screen. They rebounded off the walls of Raene's home and they echoed from the valley below. Everyone who heard Rezon's speech seemed willing to give everything they had to promote a war that had already been lost.

"Do you want TOTAL WAR?"

Screams of support from the earlier question had barely subsided when they redoubled following Rezon's request for absolute commitment. Galelian began to nurse a splitting headache.

"If necessary do you want war more total and radical than anything we can imagine today?"

Galelian retreated to the terrace, but couldn't find any place that provided shelter from the din of support for Rezon's new policy of total war. He downed several intoxicating beverages in quick succession, hoping they'd calm his pounding headache.

"Now people rise up and let the storm break loose!"

Somewhere out on Tempe Terra fireworks began to illuminate the sky. Vehicles on the highways below blew their horns and everyone in Raene's house went mad with support for a Leader who was most likely so insane he couldn't show his face in public.

Pain in Galelian's head began to create cracks in his self-restraint. He told himself this herd madness was not constructive at all, but served only to support government policy that had already failed and would ultimately destroy them all. Were people really that gullible? Apparently they were. One thing was certain. Rezon was nothing if not an able orator.

"As we this day now dedicate ourselves to winning a great war among the stars, we are reminded that we are not a people who shrink from fear of death or loss. We here today firmly

resolve to pursue Total War against our enemies both small and great until none stand between us and that which we have a right to possess.

As they have attacked us, as they have sought to make war upon us, as they continue an unmerciful struggle against us, so shall we return war upon their heads upon their worlds and upon their families. Bomb shall be met by bomb."

The presentation continued with other less able and less inspiring speakers. Testimony was given as to the ability of the people to win a war they'd only just learned had gone badly against them. People in the room talked amongst themselves in voices weakened and strained from screaming. No one would be able to speak above a whisper tomorrow.

The video concluded. Someone switched off the screen to conserve power. Dessert was offered to sweeten the taste of politics in everyone's mouth. Intoxicants flowed like a river to take the edge off a future that began to look miserable even before the last cheering echoes faded from the valley below. Rezon's speech had been memorable and everyone drank to forget what it meant.

* * *

Raene put her hand in her pocket, touched a crumpled piece of paper she'd received earlier that day, covered her face with her free hand and began to weep. Jaene, her younger sister, hurried to her side and threw an arm over Raene's shoulders. When she asked Raene what was wrong, her question was answered with a short whispered description of the paper's message. Jaene's eyes also filled with tears. Nearby, Galelian vented his opinion of the political situation and how it had become a religion of the masses.

Raene raised her tear-streaked face and asked Galelian to change the subject, "You know what they say about discussing politics and religion."

Galelian heaved a sigh, "Are you telling me to shut up about it?"

"That's what they say and you know it. It's forbidden. It's the law."

"Why? Have you asked yourself why?"

Inspired by a swollen sense of moral indignation and a little too much to drink, Galelian raised his voice a notch in volume. Some caution in the back of his mind reacted against it, but it was too late. His blood was up and the drinks he'd poured down his throat began to speak. He couldn't resist the urge to vomit his personal opinion into the evening air, "Why is there no free exchange of opinion about the direction our government is taking us? Is there no consideration for the Will of God or the possibility of establishing peace with those we've made our enemies?"

Galelian's shrill voice began to be overheard by other guests. Private conversations about current events, recipes and the antics of popular celebrities became muted. A more pervasive entertainment was at hand. Everybody paused to listen. Several guests picked up their phones and sent angry messages.

"We all know what the will of the gods is," Jaene argued. "The heavens have always sent meteors and asteroids to pummel our cities our homes and our hopes for the future. If there are gods above us they are wicked and spiteful. There's no mercy among them."

"That's ancient mythology and modern propaganda," Galelian said. "Our thoughts ought to embrace truth and Justice, not stories promoted for popular consumption. Truth addresses Justice and the morality of the One God, not self-aggrandizing religion and corrupt politicians.

The truth is that we began an unjust war against worlds beyond the stars. The truth is that WE forced them to ally themselves against us when WE attacked them without just cause. We're the ones who invaded worlds and regions not our own – to seize that which is not ours to possess. The Shundite Alliance is only defending itself against our aggression. WE are the evil party in this war, not them.

Rezon's speech has less to do with defending our way of life than it does to justify our interstellar aggression. It's about our men and women dying for an unjust cause. Its about them dying for nothing."

Raene began to sob uncontrollably.

Jaene interceded, "You're an ass Galelian. Don't you know Raene received a notice this morning from Space Service? Janian has been listed as Missing In Action. She's one of the defenders of our home world and our freedom."

Raene buried her face in Jaene's shoulder and wept.

"Janian," Galelian asked. "Who's Janian?"

"Raene's daughter, stupid. Janian is one of our best interceptor pilots."

"Right. So she's a pilot. If she's listed as Missing In Action she'll be picked up by a Search and Rescue team."

One of the other guests took Galelian by the arm and escorted him across the room into a quiet corner, "My name is John. You claim to be a journalist, but you're unusually ignorant of military matters. Don't you know interceptors have no escape pod? The craft is all weapons and engines. It doesn't even have armor. There aren't any search and rescue teams available to hunt for missing pilots – not any more. MIA is a polite way of giving citizens a false hope of seeing their sons and daughters again. If you're so interested in learning the truth of things why don't you know MIA is really a death certificate? You need to calm down, man."

Jaene and Raene retreated to a more private part of the house where the distraught mother collapsed in uncontrollable grief. On their way out, Jaene looked back over her shoulder and issued a parting suggestion in Galelian's direction, "why don't you go home before you ruin everyone's evening."

Two couples decided their good mood had already been ruined and hurriedly left for another location with a more celebratory atmosphere. Their dishes and spoons and forks were abandoned in the kitchen along with a note saying they'd come by in a few days to pick them up. They hurried out the door without so much as a good-bye to anyone. Other guests discovered how tired they'd suddenly become, but with Raene indisposed there was no one to offer polite excuses to - except the other guests. One by one and two by two they all left until no one remained except Galelian and John.

"There's nothing you can do about the political situation and you know it," John said.

"I can speak up about it and I can write about it," Galelian replied. "Things are not going well for us. There are strong indications we're losing the war. When the end comes it'll arrive so suddenly most folks won't know what hit them. We should at least be allowed to prepare ourselves for the end."

"I can't accept the possibility of defeat," John said. "Our Leader and the leaders before him have proved themselves equal to the gods in their ability to make our world secure from the destruction of the heavens as well as the Shundite Alliance."

"Our leaders aren't divine, not even close. The gods are imaginary figments of political rhetoric."

"So is your One God," John insisted.

"Is there no such thing as morality," Galelian asked. "Is it not wrong to lie cheat steal and murder? Qualities of moral law suggest a Moral Lawgiver. We stand on worthwhile principles such as duty honor and devotion to the common good. Without them society would collapse and civilization couldn't be maintained. Oh yes, there is a God. If He is the source of justice and mercy and truth, then He must be very angry with us."

"Why?"

"Because we've broken God's moral law at every point on the compass of justice and mercy. When we attacked those who did not provoke us we violated our own honor and our own laws."

"I concede our first encounters with the Shundite Alliance weren't well handled," John admitted. "But regardless of how it could've would've or should've been conducted we're now at war with them. There's nothing to be done now except to follow our Leader's orders implicitly and without question. He's our only hope."

"If he's our only hope, then we are lost - for so is he."

* * *

Galelian left Raene's dinner party a bit tipsy from food and drink and the natural high he usually got from venting his moral outrage. A car arrived to take him home, but as he prepared to enter the vehicle he thought he saw a strangely clad figure standing silently in the shadows. After seating himself in the car he looked back, but saw nothing.

He'd heard about an apparition appearing at odd times and places preaching bad news to people on Cydonia. Had he imagined what he thought he'd seen? Galelian didn't believe in such things. Perhaps it was something he'd eaten.

Galelian's ideals may have been appropriate subject matter at another time and under different circumstances, but in a climate of Total War they weren't welcome in the ears of many who heard them. Neither were they popular with the governing authorities. As he proclaimed his moral indignation that evening a warrant for Galelian's arrest was being prepared. Other departments of the global bureaucracy may have been slackened by the incompetence and corruption of endless war, but the machinations of the Cystapo remained as skilled and efficient as ever. It wouldn't be long before Galelian would learn how proficient they could be.

Chapter 11
THE CIMMERIA EXCAVATION

"Welcome to the penal colony of Hellas Planitia."

Mechanical words of recorded introduction echoed off filthy underground walls, stinging the ears and minds of a column of men who were ushered out of a cargo lift at gunpoint. The harsh announcement pierced the musty dim surroundings and focused the attention of each new prisoner on their present circumstances. As they stood in the gloom waiting for their next humiliation the sound of the cargo lifts' steel doors rang shut behind them with a chilling finality. The mechanical recording continued its impersonal announcement.

"You have been convicted of crimes against society from which you will be removed for the rest of your natural lives. You are a disease and an infection that will no longer be allowed to pollute the world above. The passage in which you are standing is one hundred ninety feet below the surface. It's the closest you will ever be allowed to approach the sky. You will never again see the face of the sun and you will never again receive communication from those you once knew. To all those who live on the surface you are now dead. You have been buried alive."

An elder inmate, who wore a trustee's armband, approached each of the new arrivals. In one hand he carried a dual-purpose branding iron and in the other he carried an electric stunner. The trustee went down the line stunning each new inmate, or fish as they were called in prison slang. One by one each fish fell to the ground. As they lay on the damp mildewed pavement thrashing like fish out of water, they were branded on their forehead and implanted with a tracking chip.

No matter where they went or how they were clothed they would forever carry a criminal's brand permanently seared into their flesh. They could not escape their new identity and they would never leave the bowels of the world into which they had been cast. At the trustee's command they painfully struggled to their feet. Galelian stood too and followed the other fish as they were led deeper into the pits of a living hell.

* * *

"We've received revised orders to extend an excavation, Master Supervisor."
"Which one, Tenicon? We're responsible for two of them."

Tenicon held out the orders. Rodion glanced at the paperwork and nodded, "I expected this. It's an order to redouble our efforts and shorten our timetable for completion of the Cimmeria excavation. We're already working on it."
"How did you know this order was coming," the younger man asked.
Rodion smiled, "Years of experience. One gets to be supervisor of a big job by anticipating leadership needs and demands. When you anticipate you can usually complete a job ahead of schedule. Didn't you hear Rezon's speech? He told us we're committed to Total War with the Shundite Alliance. That means certain projects will assume high priority. That means the Cimmeria excavation must be completed ahead of schedule as well as the long tunnel to Hellas."
"What's so important about Cimmeria?"

"I'm not exactly sure, but the Cimmeria region is where our first subterranean colleges were established. Over time they merged into a single university with a single administration."

"I know," Tenicon said. "I graduated from Cimmeria University. It's a fine institution, but what's so important about excavating there?"

Their conversation was interrupted by a group of new inmates being moved toward the excavation site. As the transport passed the two engineers Rodion recognized one of them. What's Galelian doing here, he wondered.

The Chief Engineer made a mental note to review the arrest records of new inmates when he had some free time. It was illegal for prisoners and those they once knew to have any contact with each other – above or below ground. The situation for both of them had suddenly changed. Rodion had a career and a respected position to maintain. Even the slightest commonality between the two men could prove hazardous to Rodion's reputation. The appearance of Galelian threatened everything he had worked so hard to establish.

Tenicon noticed Rodin's attention had wandered and repeated his question, "What's so important about the Cimmeria excavation, sir?"

"Sorry about that," Rodion said. ""I was considering our work here."

The Master Supervisor continued his speculation, "When the first and second Leaders promised to shelter us from the constant rain of meteors, they moved all of society underground. That was long before we learned how to fly or how to ascend into space to deal with the asteroids directly. The work we've been assigned is directly connected to shelter of some sort."

"I've read a lot of history about the asteroids," the young engineer said. "We played the space rocks like a giant game of billiards. We learned to direct a small one into a collision with a large one. The impact could be aimed to move the direction of both objects away from our world. Sometimes, if our shot was right, we could move several asteroids at once with one small rocket motor. After years of effort we steered most of the asteroids away from trajectories that would impact the surface."

"That's true," Rodion said. "When the meteor menace ended, our people returned above ground where it was easier and cheaper to build."

"Our poets artists and builders learned once again to appreciate the Great Borealis Ocean the Valles Marineris Sea and all our other seas lakes and waterways," Tenicon said. "The golden age of our industrial and cultural expansion began when newly discovered land became available."

Rodion added a caveat to their review of history, "Unfortunately that's also when we abandoned the safety of our subterranean habitations. Those ancient underground shelters are also well suited to a time of Total War. That's why I issued orders for our excavation work as soon as the Defense Minister finished his speech. He's a good speaker and an able administrator. I knew those orders would be received sooner or later. As it turns out it was sooner."

What remained unsaid were Rodion's private misgivings that it would take a great deal of time to expand the caverns to accommodate the entire population and that it would take a great deal more time to move people below ground. If the fleet situation were as severe as rumors suggested it might be, there wouldn't be enough time – not enough time at all.

Rodion knew, as many did not, their excavations couldn't begin to shelter the population below ground. His project seemed to be intended for some other purpose. He often wondered what that purpose could be.

"Why do we need to excavate additional caverns in the Cimmeria region," Tenicon asked. "Why not somewhere else where the substrata might be easier to extract?"

"I'm not sure," Rodion admitted truthfully. "An educated guess might assume additional storage space would be required for digital and virtual record storage. Cimmeria is naturally low in humidity and temperature. No special machinery would be required to preserve documents in their original condition. It's also very deep underground."

"The university administration will welcome the opportunity to increase its authority over an expanded library system," Tenicon observed.

Rodion agreed, "Academic types always welcome situations that make them look more important than they really are. As far as I'm concerned they're just glorified librarians."

"I think there's some other reason for the excavation."

"I know where you're going with that speculation," Rodion said. "It involves installing special services that storage compartments wouldn't need. We should keep such thoughts to ourselves for now. The task at hand is to make space available, not to insinuate ourselves into its purpose. Let's get to work."

Galelian's group of fish arrived at the new excavation site. Each of them was immediately put to work removing soil and rock dislodged by recent explosive charges. It was brutal dirty dangerous work and nobody would be overly concerned if an accident took a few lives in the process. Galelian bent to his task and wondered if Rodion had seen him aboard the transport with the other inmates. He wondered too whether his relationship with Rodion would be an advantage or the death of him.

Somewhere up ahead a temporary support beam collapsed dumping tons of rock and soil on workers there. Galelian heard men screaming in the darkness as limbs were torn and bones were crushed. After only a few hours into his first day of incarceration Galelian suddenly realized he was indeed a dead man. He rubbed the burnt skin on his forehead where he'd been branded. Not for the first time would he hope for a quick death.

It's been said one should be careful about what one wishes for because it may come to pass in unexpected ways.

* * *

A few weeks after his arrival at the excavation site, Galelian went missing. When a daily head count of inmates discovered his absence, a search for the absentee was begun. The searchers assumed it wouldn't take long to find him. It didn't.

The task was simple – look for the reception of an electronic return signal from a radio locater chip embedded beneath the prisoner's skin when he'd arrived at the penal colony. Searchers began their pursuit of evidence in the same area of the excavation site Galelian had been assigned work. They weren't disappointed when an electronic search signal detected his body inside a newly finished section of wall. Rules of discovery required final disposition of the case by higher authorities, meaning the searchers didn't have to exhume the body – a nasty bit of work they were glad to avoid. Galelian had gotten his wish.

Investigation of Galelian's murder then focused upon his dossier in expectation that some link would be discovered between him and his murderer. When his family association with the Chief Engineer was exposed the matter was referred to the governor for a ruling. At the same time the governor also received notification that his excavation project had been completed many days ahead of schedule and under budget. Its' success would impress the Leader and enhance the governor's political status.

The alleged crime thus became a closet scandal the governor needed to avoid. If the relationship between the murdered prisoner and his Chief Engineer became public knowledge, any political advantage that might accrue to him as a result of the success of the excavation would instantly evaporate. It would be better for the matter to remain buried – literally as well as figuratively. Therefore, Governor T'savout wisely chose to issue orders to leave the excavation site in its pristine condition – with Galelian's' dead body still entombed in the wall. As the governor's schedule of activities for the next few days included an inspection tour of the site, he decided to include a brief interview with the Chief Engineer.

Rodion was occupied with cleaning a few work tools when an unexpected guest walked into his field office.

"What are you doing, Rodion," Regional Governor T'savout asked as he strode into the room.

Surprised, Rodion dropped his tools into the sink and turned to see who had spoken, "Your Honor, this is an unexpected pleasure. I didn't expect to see you here."

"That's obvious," T'savout said - pointing to the tools in the sink. "Why are you cleaning a spade and a hammer? You have assistants to do that kind of dirty work for you."

Rodion nervously acknowledged one of the tools in the sink, "That's a commemorative silver hammer you presented to me when I was a junior student in University. I like to get it out of storage and put it on display when I'm working an important project. It's a reminder of my accomplishments – a reminder of the privilege of being granted work I enjoy."

Beads of sweat appeared on Rodion's forehead. His excuse was thin and he knew it, "I use the spade to turn the ground in each project to remind myself of the difficulties our workers have to endure."

"That's very commendable," Governor T'savout said. "I remember presenting the award to you. You were a very promising student."

Rodion's hand shook as he wiped the hammer dry with a dirty towel, "I didn't know you were coming. If I'd been informed of your visit I'd have prepared a suitable welcome."

"You might have also finished cleaning the evidence of your…work…as well," T'savout observed.

The governor cleared his throat and continued, "The fact you've completed the Cimmeria excavation project under budget and ahead of schedule is welcome enough. Our Leader is aware of your achievement and asked me to convey his congratulations to you on its success. It promises to aid the war effort immensely."

Rodion offered the governor a seat next to his desk, "may I order a refreshment, sir?"

"This isn't a social call, Rodion. I could use a rest, though. I've been walking a lot today. My doctor says its good for me, but my knees disagree."

The governor sat heavily in a nearby chair. Obvious relief showed on his face.

"I appreciate your visit today sir. May I ask if there's anything I can do for you?"

"I'm walking these dismal corridors to conduct an inspection tour. New equipment has been installed in the excavation site and I've been asked to certify it for operation. It's more ceremonial than technical because I haven't the slightest idea how it's supposed to work. The purpose of my unscheduled visit with you is to make certain you understand your position in the scheme of things.

As an expression of our Leader's confidence in your abilities, I've been instructed to inform you that you will be awarded several projects like the Cimmeria excavation in the near future. These special excavations will be used to build and operate a new type of weapon, which our Leader believes will turn the tide of war in our favor. At present we have only two working prototypes, including the one here in Cimmeria. We need dozens – perhaps hundreds more like them to defeat our enemies."

"We shall endeavor to continue to fulfill our Leader's confidence in us," Rodion said.

The governor stood to his feet and prepared to leave, "I hope so Master Supervisor."

He glanced briefly into the sink, part of which was still smeared with bloodstains from the tool cleaning. Rodion swallowed hard as he watched the governor study the stains. His deed had been discovered and he knew it.

"Your efficiency is a state asset," the governor said as he turned to go. "You should understand at this point that instead of the award of a medal or certificate of appreciation for this project your reward will be an extension of your license to continue unimpeded with your service to Cydonia. Have I made myself clear?"

Rodion was visibly shaking when he said he understood the governor's meaning.

"That's good, very good. Perhaps you'll be granted commendations in the future if you continue your good work and keep your tools clean. Guard your future actions and words Master Supervisor. You still have a bright future. Be careful not to ruin it."

"Thank you, sir," Rodion said as the governor disappeared into the passageway outside his office.

His heart was still pounding when he finished cleaning the sink and his tools. A smudge of blood remained on T'savout's commemorative hammer. Rodion wiped it clean with a dry towel and hid it deep inside a cabinet. Good fortune had smiled on him, he told himself. There would be time enough to collect awards later.

Somewhere in the depths of his heart a still small voice echoed an old proverb, which said if you want to make God laugh you should tell Him your plans.

Chapter 12
BAPTISM OF FIRE

Armed guards sealed every access to Tempe Terra spaceport. Top Secret activity was in progress. Imposed restrictions recognized the possibility of eavesdropping or sabotage even though the general population supported every decision the government made. Loaded and installed within the redesigned cargo hold of a high capacity warp transport was a device so new it's builders hadn't had time to paint it or properly label it's buttons and switches. Its hatches were sealed as guards watched. A few minutes later ground control cleared it for immediate launch.

Raene, wife of Chief Engineer Rodion and aggrieved mother of Space Service interceptor pilot Janian, had lost another battle with insomnia and wearily plodded to the terrace outside her home. During an evening phone call Rodion had informed her he'd completed an important project and would be allowed some well-earned vacation time at home. Her mind raced with the possibilities of seeing him again. She tried to make herself comfortable in her old lounge chair, but realized its lumps and sagging padding might soon require a replacement.

Out on the planitia a speck of light, larger than most, brightened suddenly and launched into the air with the speed of summer lightning. Raene watched it make a few circles in the sky until it disappeared through its interspatial transit point. I wonder where it went and what exotic ports of call it will visit, she thought.

A parsec from its launch point the refitted transport reappeared in normal space above one of Cydonia's last planetary outposts. It joined three interceptors already on station and assumed the hindmost position in a diamond formation. The three interceptors were all that remained in a sector that once counted them in the hundreds. Ahead and above them, an invasion fleet of the Shundite Alliance slowed its approach and prepared for battle.

* * *

Claxons shrieked and warning lights blazed in every war room on the home world and beyond - notifying military personnel they should man their battle stations. War alerts had been issued a few days previously, but this time it was for real. This was no drill. An enemy fleet had appeared. Hostilities were about to commence.

Several levels below ground in the Pentagon Situation Room, the Leader seated himself at the head of a conference table. He sipped a mild intoxicant as his new military advisors cautiously joined him in their chairs. He'd been drinking regularly since his mental breakdown and everyone knew it. Not sure as to how the Leader would react to new events, each of them had vacillated between absence and personal safety on one hand and curiosity about new weapons on the other.

In the end curiosity outweighed concerns for personal safety as the Leader's staff waited and watched for the effects of new weapons as they were deployed in battle for the first time. It was almost like waiting for the detonation of the first atomic bomb. Everyone had been told what to expect, but actually watching the thing do its hideous work was something nobody wanted to miss.

Two identical devices had been installed on the home world – one buried deep inside the Pentagon. On the other side of the planet, the second device had been fitted over nine hundred feet below ground level at the University of Cimmeria. The principle feature of each facility was a single room occupied by three men and a strange new machine. Several levels below the

Situation Room, technicians prepared to arm and energize a device they hoped would turn the tide of war in their favor.

* * *

Sev 'Olen had been born and raised on a farm in the southern highlands of the Home World. His family had been farmers for generations, but Sev's heart was never interested in growing things or nurturing livestock. From the earliest years of his youth he'd imagined himself at the controls of a powerful interceptor as it flew among the stars – defending his family and friends from enemies both natural and alien.

Each day, when the usual boring hours of required schooling were completed, Sev would find ways to study everything he could find about interceptor battle tactics, engine mechanics, stellar navigation, weapon systems and even the history of the uniforms the pilots wore. He pinned star charts on his bedroom wall and if a girl friend, who had different stars in her eyes, couldn't find a particular constellation in the night sky he'd tell her something about its legend and which season of the year it would reappear. He was an attractive kid, as farm kids go, and suffered no lack of young ladies who were more than willing to endure astronomical lectures in exchange for a few hours of his company.

When he entered Space Service Academy Sev knew more than most instructors. Graduation at the head of his class came as no surprise to anyone as well as his predictable promotion to Flight Leader status. Sev was really that good at what he'd dreamed of doing. The day after graduation he shipped out to his first duty assignment.

On Meribah, one of the last planetary outposts of the Cydonian Empire, Sev began training his Flight crews for a special assignment – integration with a new type of space weapon. An invasion alert from Cydonia Command cut their training short, but found him and his pilots combat ready nonetheless. The interceptors were prepped and armed. Each pilot was ready for new challenges at a moment's notice. That moment wasn't long in coming.

Originally designed and deployed as a high-speed freighter, Shield Ship One dropped into normal space and assumed the tail position of a diamond formation with Sev and his two wingmen. As it sailed into position a shimmering purple bubble of energy emanated from its hull – enveloping itself and the three interceptors ahead of it. The combined formation was prepared to deliver the approaching Shundite fleet a deadly surprise.

Fifteen Shundite fighters broke off from the main fleet with the intention of rendering Sev's smaller flight group into space junk. Sev ordered one of his wingmen to accelerate with him to meet the approaching Shundite fighters while the remaining interceptor remained in reserve with the Shield Ship. As they accelerated away from the original diamond formation, parts of the purple shield bubble went with them – providing mobile protection. Interceptors were smaller faster and much more maneuverable than Shundite fighters because none of them had ever flown into battle with armor or shielding. This time the engagement would be different. To say Shundite Fighter Command was surprised would be an understatement.

Shundite fighters fired the first shots of the skirmish from maximum range – an advantage of distance the heavier fighters enjoyed over the smaller interceptors. A full volley of energy weapons was directed at Sev and his wingman in the expectation the fusillade would end the fight before it began. It didn't.

Instead of being disintegrated the two interceptors plowed on – surrounded and protected by their strange new purple shielding. Sev and his wingman closed to striking range. Bobbing and weaving among the enemy fighters, they managed to destroy or disable five of them on their first pass through the enemy formation. Executing a tight Delta V maneuver both interceptors reversed course and proceeded to press their attack upon the invaders from behind. Shundite fighter pilots reacted by breaking up their formation. A general melee began.

It was a true dogfight in every sense of the word. Shundite fighters rolled turned dove and climbed as best they could, but were no match for the more maneuverable Cydonian interceptors. Every Shundite weapon that struck an interceptor failed to damage them. The two invulnerable interceptors closed to point blank range on the fighters and caused heavy damage every time they fired at one. One by one and in rapid succession the two interceptors destroyed or disabled every fighter sent against them – absorbing direct hits with their new shielding and meting out punishment upon the opposing squadron that surprised observers on both sides.

Cydonian interceptors didn't suffer as much as a ding on their paint jobs. Both retired to their original diamond formation to await the enemies' next move and to recharge their offensive weapons. The Shundite fleet, undaunted by the defeat of their fighters, continued to approach Meribah and the four ships that protected it. Sev requested permission to interdict the larger Shundite bombers and troop carriers, but approval was denied.

Shield Ship engineers had discovered a problem with the shield emitter system and were forced to reduce power by eighty-five percent. Insufficient power would be available to project shielding around the interceptors if they ventured beyond the Shield Ship's formation. Sev sat in his spacecraft and pounded the instrument panel with his fists in frustration. He and his wingman had executed the most successful interceptor sortie in recent history and were now powerless to do anything more than to silently sit and watch the approaching Shundite fleet. On the home world, in the bowels of the Pentagon, the Leader would order the use of something special for both Sev and his enemies to watch.

* * *

In the Situation Room of the Pentagon, The Leader jumped to his feet and joyfully proclaimed the superiority of Cydonian power, "This is a great victory, a very great victory. Our interceptors have defended us with honor against greater numbers and won the day. We haven't seen such a triumph in years. It proves what I've believed all along. Our technology and our people are more resilient and more resourceful than any possible adversary. This is a great victory.   It's a great day for all of us."

The Military Chief of Staff agreed, "You're preaching to the choir, my Leader. This is only the beginning.   The enemy has seen nothing yet of our ability to carry the fight to them."

A junior member of the staff dared to voice caution, "Today's achievement by Interceptor Command is a very real encouragement, but we must remind ourselves that the new shield system is far from being fully deployed. The Shield Ship on station at Meribah is the only one we have in operation. We should be conservative in its use and cautious with our expectations."

The Leader refused to hear the words of the younger officer. Bloated with pride at the initial success he screamed with delight, "Our enemy will rue the day they dared to raise their hands against us. Our brave pilots have risen to the challenge of superior numbers and have defeated them all. Nothing can stop us now."

"May I order the release of our primary weapon," the Chief of Staff asked.

"So ordered," the Leader shouted. "Let their mouths be filled with the taste of their own blood. Let their eyes watch as their fleet is reduced to ashes."

The junior officer kept his silence. This is a very great mistake, he thought. The primary weapon system is still experimental.

The Leader ordered another intoxicant, a stronger one than his first, and returned to his seat to watch the outcome of the next stage of their defensive plan. He was absolutely convinced of its success and imagined himself delivering a victory speech to his people after dinner.

* * *

Beneath the Cydonia Pentagon and under the University of Cimmeria crews of three technicians at each site sealed themselves inside specially designed bombproof chambers. Each chamber contained a new secret weapon called an Interocitor. In theory, an Interocitor could incinerate a pencil on a nearby table as easily as it could destroy an enormous battle cruiser in space hundreds of parsecs away. It could also be used to call a restaurant on the other side of town to order delivery of a sandwich for lunch. It was an all-purpose weapon and communications device that could theoretically win the war against the Shundite Alliance. The Leader was boastful and confident of its potential, but many scientists and several military experts entertained quiet doubts. The system wasn't fully tested and most certainly untried under battle conditions.

The primary operators of each Interocitor seated themselves at their respective machines and donned a skullcap that served as an interface between the machine and its living counterpart. It was connected to the shaven head of its operator by means of tiny screws and wires that were painfully embedded into the operator's scalp. A second technician, who acted as a redundant operator, wore an identical skullcap interface. In the event of an electro-biological malfunction that killed or incapacitated the primary operator, the second tech would assume control of the machine.

Manipulation of an Interocitor was so dangerous that many trainees had died during their first attempt to use one. Interocitor Control had insisted upon procedures that required two operators as well as a third technician to be present in the chamber during any test, battle drill or engagement of its lethal capabilities.

The third person in an Interocitor control room was an experienced electrical engineer who could perform adjustments and repairs as necessary. He was also responsible to safely and rapidly shut down the machine in the event its operation went awry, it had killed both operators or was about to explode. An Interocitor was an extremely volatile piece of equipment, which is why it had to be buried in the ground hundreds of feet from inhabited sections of a city or a command site. No medical personnel were present because it was assumed any accident would be instantly fatal to the Interocitor team.

Interocitor Control relayed the Pentagon command to release the weapons for operation against the Shundite invasion fleet. Upon acknowledging the order each Interocitor team was instructed to fire at will. When the operation commenced all previous space weapon systems became obsolete.

The primary operator of the Pentagon Interocitor stiffened in his seat as the machine's interface engaged his brain. Tiny wisps of smoke emanated from two of the probes screwed into his scalp. Ready for such an eventuality, the engineer made a few quick adjustments to voltage and current levels – allowing the operator to relax. He thought they'd be good to go, but something about the machine's performance didn't seem quite right. All settings and readings were nominal, but something smelled rotten about it – literally. The primary operator settled into his task and began his deadly work, but somewhere in the complex innards of the machine the insulation surrounding its quantum connectors began to smolder under the load of current.

* * *

In stationary orbit around Meribah, Sev's nerves wore thin. He'd been ordered to stand down for the time being, but sitting in his interceptor watching the Shundite fleet approach unopposed wasn't how he thought the enemy should be greeted, especially when he and his wingman had proved they could inflict severe damage on their fighters. Sev broke radio silence and demanded a status report from the Shield Ship.

"Unchanged at this time, sir."

"What do you mean unchanged? I'm sitting here watching the enemy approach. If we're going to defend this outpost we need to do something. I need to know what's going on. What's your status?"

"We've tested the shield system and found the reactor in perfect working order. Shield emitters are nominal as well."

"Understood, so why can't we get going?"

"Power conduits are overheated. The power coupling from the reactor to the emitters is dangerously overheated. We're barely maintaining formation shielding at 16% power. The cooling system isn't rated for battle stress."

"I was told before we came on station that everything had been tested and was combat ready," Sev said.

"It was tested, but not under battle conditions. Enemy hits on the shielding caused an overload of the power conduit. The cooling system isn't rated for that much pressure. We need time to allow it to cool off."

"Are you telling me we have to just sit here and watch Shundite ships pour into orbit?"

"We're working on it sir, but our best estimate is twelve to fifteen hours before power conduit temperatures cool enough to risk another engagement. Ideally we should have several Shield Ships with accompanying interceptors for an engagement like this."

"Well, we don't have that many ships do we? What would happen if we tried to attack the enemy anyway," Sev asked.

"If the power coupling blows we'll lose all shielding. We'll be exposed to Shundite attack."

At that moment a long range unmanned object, launched from the closest Shundite ship, struck the shield bubble and exploded. No damage was recorded, but Sev was told the attack had reduced shield power by 2%.

Sev yelled into his microphone, "We have to do something. We can't just sit here and get whittled down to nothing."

At that moment something did happen. Long-range sensors on Sev's control panel registered a large energy emission from the ship that had just launched an attack against them.

Sev's wingman voiced surprise on their communicator circuit, "Did you pick that up?"

"I did," Sev acknowledged. "And I just saw another one farther out."

"What's going on?"

"If I didn't know better I'd say two of the Shundite ships just exploded."

"How's that possible? We didn't do it. Are there other interceptors in this sector?"

"None I'm aware of. We're all that's available."

Sev studied his long-range display with renewed interest and watched another Shundite ship become a miniature star.

"Shield Ship command center, this is Flight Leader. What's happening to the Shundite fleet?"

"This is Shield command. We've received a notification from Interocitor Control. They have informed us the primary weapons are being deployed against the Shundite fleet. We've been asked to stand by."

Sev's wingman broke into the communication, "What's Interocitor Control, Flight Leader?"

"It's a secret," Sev said as another Shundite ship exploded. A second smaller explosion followed a few seconds later.

"It would've been nice if someone had told us to expect it," the wingman said.

"That's why they call it a secret," Sev answered. "Looks like a smaller ship was caught in that last blast. That was a secondary explosion. I wonder what an Interocitor is. How do they do that?"

The communicators of all three interceptors announced an observation from the Shield Ship, "The Shundite fleet appears to have reversed course. Another of their ships has exploded. That makes six of them so far."

"They're withdrawing," Sev's wingman hollered. "We've beaten them. We've won."

Sev wasn't so confident. "I'm glad they're pulling away," he told his wingman. "But they may just be moving off to regroup for another attack. We need to be watchful and ready."

Sev next contacted the shield ship, "The situation has changed. Contact Cydonia Command and request orders for further action. Shall we hold here or attack or withdraw?"

A long silence followed Sev's request. Sev asked again, but again there was no response. After a third request for orders he received a strange reply from the Shield Ship, "Cydonia Command at the Pentagon isn't responding. We've received a strange message from Phobos Station informing us they'll be relaying messages from now on. No new orders have come in and no one is responding to our requests for information or orders. The Pentagon has gone silent."

Long-range sensors aboard the Shield Ship detected no new explosions in the region of the Shundite fleet, which had apparently halted its withdrawal.

"They're definitely regrouping, Flight Leader," Shield Ship command reported. "Long range sensors have detected changes in the formations of their ships."

"Any news from Phobos Station or Cydonia Command?"

Another long pause followed. Sev began to get concerned about the lack of communication from Cydonia. Why was everything suddenly so quiet?

"Flight Leader, this is Shield Ship communications. Phobos has relayed a message from Interocitor control stating their systems are down. What do you recommend?"

"I don't know what an Interocitor is, but if they're down that doesn't sound good."

"We repeat our request Flight Leader. What action do you recommend?"

"We can't defend Meribah in our present condition. We can't stay here and we have no orders to do anything else. If Interocitor Control had something to do with those explosions and if they're out of action, then we're on our own."

No new orders were received from Cydonia. Phobos Station couldn't acknowledge they'd successfully relayed Sev's report of conditions in his sector to any command on the home world. Something had gone very wrong. The young Flight Leader realized that if the meager forces under his command were to survive and fight another day they'd have to withdraw. He didn't like it and he didn't want it, but there it was – a tough situation requiring a hard decision.

Sev knew his next words would change the course of his career if not the status of the war in that sector, "In my opinion and on my authority we need to preserve the ships we have with us. Prepare to jump to a secure sector. Unless we hear from somebody in command we're pulling out. Notify Phobos Station. Execute withdrawal when ready."

Sev sat in his interceptor and watched as the Shield Ship and his two wingmen flicked out of normal space. His long-range sensors recorded the renewed approach of the Shundite fleet as he prepared for his own jump to safety. His hand hovered over the instrument panel. All systems were go for the jump. Like captains of sinking ships of the past who were the last ones to abandon ship, Sev would be the last to yield the space they'd defended.

It had been a day for the record books. In spite of the most impressive tactical victory in history fought without a single loss, Sev's flight group was in full retreat. New technology had been tried successfully in battle, but it had been too little and too late. The battle of Meribah had been lost.

Sev's interceptor disappeared from normal space as the Shundite fleet prepared to enter orbit unopposed. They'd suffered humiliating losses, but they'd won. None of their commanders congratulated themselves because they were as confused about their victory as Sev was about the retreat he'd been forced to order.

Chapter 13
THE LAST DANCE

Beneath Cydonia's massive five-sided pyramid, commonly known as the Pentagon, its military command and communication centers buzzed with excited activity. A mere two interceptors had defeated an entire Shundite fighter squadron without loss of life or a single hit on their spacecraft. The new shield system had problems, but it'd worked under battle conditions. Interceptor Command was impressed beyond words. Inside the Situation Room, built deep inside the Pentagon, the Leader was overjoyed. His pride swelled and his ego erupted as though he'd done the deed himself.

The Great Man screamed with delight, "Our enemy will rue the day they dared to raise their hands against us. Our brave pilots have risen to the challenge of superior numbers and have defeated them all. Nothing can stop us now."

"May I order the release of our primary weapon," the Chief of Staff asked.

"So ordered," the Leader shouted. "Let their mouths be filled with the taste of their own blood. Let their eyes watch as their fleet is reduced to ashes."

The Leader ordered a strong intoxicating beverage, downed it in a single swallow and ordered another as he returned to his seat. If the outcome of the next stage of the defensive plan was only half as successful as his scientists predicted he'd become a living legend among his people. Convinced of its success, he saw himself veiled in majesty and clothed in immense power as he delivered the first of many victory speeches to his people later that evening.

From its sparkling new facility at Cimmeria, Interocitor Control relayed the Pentagon order to its two teams. Inside sealed chambers at Cimmeria and below the Pentagon Situation Room each Interocitor operator received an identical command. It was composed of three simple words, "Engage the weapon."

* * *

Interocitors operated on a level of quantum mechanics that made a joke of previously understood laws of physics. Distance wasn't a factor in the transmission of messages or destructive power.

Years earlier it had been discovered that certain properties of matter in the quantum state allowed instantaneous communication over vast distances. It was called Quantum Communication and it made the long distance use of radio obsolete. Gone were the restrictions of common radio frequency transmissions that could take hours or days or weeks to reach a receiver. Gone were the days when an enemy could interdict or tap into a communication. The communications network of the Cydonian Empire had long employed Quantum Communications to allow efficient and instant messaging between its distant planets outposts and vessels.

Unfortunately, the use of Quantum Communications had its drawbacks. Despite its enormous enhancement of military communications its misuse resulted in the general degradation of society's private sector. Pornography in many forms became rampant among those stationed in lonely outposts. Commercial transactions threatened to overload the network and often did. Social media reduced productive loyal star systems to whining rebellious clusters of illiterate unproductive mutineers. After two entire star systems seceded from the Empire and joined the Shundite Alliance, all social media was forbidden all commercial transactions were limited and all defamatory rhetoric about the Leader became a criminal offense.

The ultimate military developmental step in quantum mechanics allowed the transmission of destructive power over any distance. Theoretically, it was as easy to incinerate a book a few feet from an Interocitor console, as it was to destroy an enemy battle cruiser many parsecs distant. The problem with quantum energy displacement was that a huge reservoir of energy was required at the initiating site. An Interocitor didn't create energy. It was a transducer that could direct available energy upon any target at any distance in any amount. Because of its potentially limitless power consumption, an Interocitor was a very dangerous piece of equipment to operate.

Mental integration was the final step in the deployment of the Interocitor weapon system. Instead of using dials and pushbuttons or a complex computer program, the machine was manipulated directly by means of a physical interface with an operator's brain.

Months of training and mental discipline preceded a candidate's first attempt at operating an Interocitor. It was usually fatal. More than ninety percent of those who tried it died instantly. The majority of those who didn't die had their brains trashed and lived the rest of their lives as mouth-breathing droolers – suitable only as contenders for political office or in positions as managers of the bloated bureaucracy. Only one percent of those who began the training succeeded. Of those who survived their first attempt to operate the device, many were discovered to have had their intelligence quotient permanently doubled or tripled.

Advertisements requesting volunteers for a secret training program suggested its graduates would have their cerebral abilities enhanced to the level of Super-Genius. It never mentioned the possibility they stood a good chance of being reduced to the mental equivalent of bacteria. Graduates would forever be considered children of the universe, the adverts claimed, because although they'd been born with physical bodies they could acquire the powers of demi-gods. It was all utter nonsense of course, but it proved to be an effective myth to recruit volunteers who would most likely die from the experience. The failure rate was never reported to the general population – a deliberate oversight nearly discovered by a young investigative journalist named Galelian.

* * *

Power was applied to the Interocitor console at the Pentagon site – immediately resulting in an accidental overload that nearly fried the operator's brain. The odor of burning flesh drifted into the air. Tiny curls of smoke emanated from two metal screws embedded in his scalp. On the verge of electrocution, his body stiffened from the current passing through it. The engineer, who was poised at the controls, immediately reduced the current load - allowing the operator to relax and concentrate on operating the machine. Precious minutes would be lost as the operator fought to recover from the shock and regain his concentration.

At the newer Cimmeria site, console initialization proceeded flawlessly. The primary operator got to work and quickly discovered the Shield Ship and its interceptors had come under attack. Focusing his attention on the Shundite vessel that had launched the attack, he activated the weapon sequence. In his mind's eye he saw the Shundite vessel as though he was swimming in space only a hundred yards away from its hull. He reached out with his mind and focused every ounce of hatred and enmity in his being at the Shundite vessel. The Interocitor hummed with a surge of directed energy and projected it through quantum space at the targeted object. It exploded instantly.

Interocitor control sent a short notification to the Pentagon Situation Room, "Enemy ship targeted and destroyed."

A video monitor on the wall of the Situation Room relayed long-range sensor data from the Shield Ship - showing a flare of energy from the direction of the Shundite fleet. The Leader clapped his hands like a delighted school child. It was an awesome display of pure destructive power. Several of the military leaders seated at the table next to him smiled with relief. A few of them didn't.

One of them, an engineer who'd begun to sweat profusely, whispered to the man next to him, "It isn't over yet."

"What do you mean?"

"Power conduits in this building are ancient. They can't handle a sustained demand for power from the Interocitor."

"What are you talking about? Test firing at meteors and asteroids went perfectly."

"Not perfectly, not even once. Test results revealed unsteady fluctuations in this building's power supply. It happened every time. Each time we were able to shut down the equipment without damage," the engineer said. He wiped the sweat off his brow with a shaking hand, "I don't think we should push our luck. We can't sustain an attack. Evidence suggests a catastrophic failure is inevitable. We need more testing and inspection of the power conduits."

"You're being defeatist," his companion said. "If you're so nervous about it why don't you head down to Power Central and monitor the equipment."

"That's a good idea," the engineer said.

He quietly excused himself and left the Situation Room, but as soon as the door closed behind him he ran, literally sprinting, for the nearest exit.

The Pentagon Interocitor team reported they were ready for action and were informed by Interocitor Control to fire at will. Eager to make up for lost time the operator located a large Shundite battle cruiser near the rear of the invasion formation and focused his destructive power on it. The Interocitor responded with a loud hum as it consumed all available power and directed it through quantum space at the target. The battle cruiser exploded instantly.

In the Pentagon, power systems jittered from the Interocitor's demand for energy. All the lights dimmed in every office, hallway and equipment bay. The engineer, who'd left the Situation Room at a dead run, was still in the building when it happened. He knew the reduced capacity of the power regulators and what the unusual strain upon them would cause. Fear of the results of another surge drove him forward. In a state of utter panic he flung himself through an outer door.

Inside the Interocitor console, most of the protective layer of insulation had burned away from critical quantum connections. The innards of the machine began to spark and fizzle, which in turn caused severe fluctuations of the Interocitor power indicators. The safety engineer seated at the console noticed them, but did nothing about it. It was a concern, but one he attributed to the building's power supply rather than any problem with the machine itself. It would prove to be a fatal misjudgment. The building's power surge had caused severe damage to the Interocitor's own internal power supply. The machine should have been shut down, but political pressure from leaders in the Situation Room, who expected performance rather than caution, would lead to an inevitable catastrophic failure.

Not to be outdone, the Cimmeria Interocitor team located their second Shundite target of the day and released deadly energy toward the vessel. It exploded like a miniature Supernova.

The destruction being unleashed upon the enemy was no longer a secret to anyone – friend or foe. At that point, Interocitor control sent a message to the Shield Ship stating their weapons were being deployed against the Shundite fleet. The source of the message was more of a surprise and more cryptic to those who received it than the explosions themselves. It was the first time the word Interocitor had been used by anyone other than those involved in the secret project.

Every successful burst of energy visible on the long-range monitor screen in the Pentagon Situation Room meant another Shundite vessel had been blown to bits. Cheering and backslapping became contagious as everyone including the Leader savored the tremendous damage being inflicted upon the Shundite invasion fleet.

Outside the building, the truant engineer burst out of the last door. In his mad rush to escape he knocked a junior officer to the ground. The panicked engineer spun around to regain his balance and continued running, neither pausing nor slowing to apologize to anyone for his actions. Puffing wheezing and suffering leg cramps, he ran like a man who'd completely lost his mind. The junior officer stood to his feet and dusted himself off. What's his problem, he wondered. If he'd known he'd have started running too.

The Pentagon Interocitor operator discovered two Shundite ships unusually close to one another - embedded deep inside the fleet formation. Both were sheltered from external attack, except the Interocitor of course. Perhaps they're exchanging crew or spare parts, the operator speculated. Maybe they're taking on food or water. Whatever reason they might have had for being so close together it would prove fatal for both of them.

Both ships swam into view of his mind's eye as the operator focused the Interocitors' targeting system on the larger of the two vessels. Neither sympathy nor compassion diluted his determination to focus every iota of hatred and bitter fury at the enemy. Once again a loud hum was heard in the Interocitor control room as the machine demanded and directed an unprecedented amount of power through quantum space at the objective. The target detonated, but with a magnitude of energy much greater than anything previously projected by an Interocitor. Its resulting blast wave penetrated and surrounded the space occupied by the nearby ship. Moments later it too exploded, but inside the Interocitor console the last bit of quantum insulation failed. A cascade failure of one component after another incinerated the control and safety mechanisms of the deadliest machine ever invented. The Interocitor exploded.

The Leader was literally dancing around the Situation Room and screaming at the top of his lungs, "A great day, a great day, a very great day. I am the greatest Leader this world has ever seen."

The dual explosion of two Shundite ships surprised even those who watched the event on the view screen.

"That ought to do it," the Military Chief of Staff declared. "They'll start running now."

He was partly right. On the view screen the Shundite fleet's reversal of course seemed to indicate a general retreat as the Cimmeria Interocitor cremated a sixth ship.

The Leader, still dancing around the table, shouted with pride and arrogance, "They can't defeat us now. Ultimate victory is ours. I'm the god of war and I'll destroy them all."

Those were the last words the Leader would ever speak.

Cydonian culture had become enamored of its own technology and its own accomplishments. Over the years the traditional ideas and myths and rules that had formed the glue of society had been replaced by a toxic form of hedonistic repression. The last vestige of a sane appraisal of his personal place in the universe melted away when the Leader claimed the status of a deity. He didn't just say it. On the day Shundite warships burned in space he and the people around him believed it too.

Filled with their own self-importance and arrogance, the Leader and his staff celebrated their greatest victory as death approached on quantum wings.

* * *

Extreme demands for power burned away the last remaining portions of safety insulation surrounding the Pentagon Interocitor's quantum circuits. A short circuit resulted, which in turn combined the machines' quantum energy state with the almost unlimited destructive potential of the nuclear reactor that provided electricity to the building. The Interocitor suddenly had access to all the power it needed to destroy itself, the building and everything in it. In moments, the explosion's concussive shock wave demolished every level separating the Interocitor Control room from the Situation Room. Everyone and every thing in the Pentagon was incinerated or crushed by the collapse of its internal structures.

The five-sided pyramid known popularly as the Pentagon had been designed and built centuries earlier in the hope it would provide a modicum of protection from meteors that fell from the sky. In time it became the seat of political and military power as well as one of the symbols of the Cydonian Empire.

Although its basic design allowed for protection from outside, its inner surface acted like a parabolic dish upon the energy released by the explosive force of the Interocitor. Terra-watts of expanding energy blasted the interior of the structure and were focused downward into the subsurface strata of the ground below its foundations – creating a colossal earthquake.

The Pentagon earthquake was so powerful it would be felt on the opposite side of the planet and register on seismic instruments at Cimmeria University. Polished white stones that formed a gleaming façade on the outside of the pyramid loosened and cracked from the shock. Cover stones from one entire side of the pyramid collapsed into a heap on the ground.

A small city had been established in the shadow of The Face when the Third Leader commissioned its sculpture. Workers and artisans from every district on the planet made their homes in its streets. When the five-sided pyramid was established as the political and military center of planetary administration, that same city grew in size to accommodate engineers, technicians, politicians, military leaders and all their families. The day the Interocitor exploded and created its great earthquake every building in the city was destroyed. Thousands perished when great towers of glass and adamantine steel folded from the shock and fell to the ground. In time, only the ancient stone foundations of the original town would remain.

Interocitor Control, located in the Cimmeria province, registered warnings on its equipment – triggered by the earthquake shocks. Caution was considered an appropriate course of action and a temporary halt of Interocitor discharges was ordered. Messages were dispatched to all sectors stating the system was down, but none that were sent to the Pentagon were acknowledged as received – not even by automatic equipment. No one knew the extent of the damage caused by the Interocitor explosion. No one would know anything for days.

* * *

The dynasty of the World Leader had ended after nearly five hundred years of oppressive rule. The battle of Meribah proved to be the last gasp of the Cydonian Empire. Never again would their military power oppress neighboring star systems. Despite every tactical victory imaginable the strategic advantage, as well as the war, had been lost.

The final act on the stage of Cydonian history remained to be played. When their enemies delivered it, the curtain would come down on any possibility of Cydonian ascendency to power in any imaginable future. Even the ghosts of its civilization would eventually wither into extinction.

Chapter 14
APOCALYPSE

Reflections of the distant sun glittered off the waves of the Great Borealis Ocean 3,700 miles beneath the rookie's optical display. Vladian studied his home planet intensely - memorizing its every feature, clinging to a fading hope that its beauty would endure. The enemy was coming and no one, especially a raw rookie aboard an orbiting observation station, knew what would happen when they arrived.

A weather front moved slowly toward the Mensae shore promising to deliver seasonal rain to the thirsty ground. The observer returned to his unfinished weather report and typed a few extra lines. When broadcast to receiving stations on the surface, it would predict an average day on the blue-green planet. Among those who would benefit from his report was Vladian's uncle. Somewhere on the ocean beneath his gaze, the old man still made his living plying the shipping lanes - still in love with the sea.

Uncle Modion had spent his life as a merchant seaman aboard ships of every size and type. On those rare occasions when the sailor took shore leave to visit brother Rodion's family, he'd regale his young nephew with exciting stories about storms at sea and exotic ports of call. The old sea dog claimed he'd visited every harbor on the Borealis Ocean as well as the entire length of Valles Marineris and back again - repeatedly. His stories, as well as the unusual presents he brought from far away places, had set Vladian's youthful imagination ablaze, but instead of sailing on the ocean the boy dreamed of becoming a mariner of the sky. Vladian hoped to seek his own adventures among the stars.

His first assignment above the atmosphere was his present duty as weather observer and communications specialist aboard the orbiting platform Phobos Station. The novice observer focused his concentration on the weather patterns below, unaware of the entry of a silent visitor into his cramped observation chamber.

The Station Chief made a pretense of clearing his throat so as to get Vladian's attention. The young man turned and stood to attention.

"I've just received an encrypted message from Ground Command," the Chief said.

The older man paused a moment, unwilling to deliver the unwelcome news he carried. He glanced at the optical display of the planet's surface and breathed a deep sigh, "It's a beautiful world down there isn't it?"

"Yes sir. It's the best. May I ask the nature of the message?"

The Chief paused and then asked why Vladian was composing a weather report.

"My relief is late for his watch. The report needs to go out, so I'm finishing it."

"Ic'abod's been late several times hasn't he?"

"He's had a lot of things on his mind since the Leader died."

"We've all been affected by his death, but that's no excuse to abandon our duties. We depend on each other up here. The world depends on our reports and communications relays. Where is he?"

"Not sure, chief. He may be in the airlock."

"The airlock? Why would he hang out there?"

"He says it's his only private place on the station. He's been spending a lot of time there."

Two lights on the indicator panel changed colors and caught the Chief's eye, "Why is he securing the airlock's inner door and unlocking the outer door?"

"I don't know why he'd do that," Vladian admitted. "He hasn't done that before."

The Chief turned and ran from the observation chamber, "Stay here until I get back."

Where else would I go, Vladian asked himself.

* * *

At the airlock, the Station Chief activated the intercom, "What do you think you're doing Ic'abod? You need to relieve Vladian. It's your watch."

At first there was no answer. Ic'abod stared out the outer door's small window at the home world below.

"It's a beautiful world isn't it Chief?"

"It's the best, now come out of there."

"Can't do that, Chief. Time's almost up."

"What in the name of the Leader are you talking about?"

Ic'abod turned around to face the Chief through the window of the inner door, "That's just the point isn't it Chief? There isn't any Leader any more, is there?"

"We'll find a new one Ic'abod. Until then you need to assume your duties."

"With all due respect Chief, I don't believe we'll find a new one – not in time anyway."

"Not in time for what," the Chief asked.

Tears were streaming down Ic'abod's face, "You know what's about to happen. The Shundite Alliance is coming. When they get here our beautiful world will end."

"You need to come out of there and assume your post," the Chief hollered.

Ic'abod turned back to the outer door, "What's the point, Chief? What difference does it make? Our Great Leader is dead and all the brilliant men who could lead us against our enemies died with him. It's only a matter of time before that beautiful world down there is wrecked. Isn't it better to remember it the way it is now? Isn't it better to end the struggle while its still a beautiful thing to behold?"

"Listen to me," the Chief said. "We'll find a way out of this. We always do."

"Not this time," Ic'abod said between deep sobs. "We've committed unspeakable atrocities against people who could've been our friends. Now they're against us because we betrayed them, because we took what wasn't ours to take and killed those who hadn't attacked us. They're justified in their rage and they're coming to have vengeance upon us. I've seen the reports, Chief. So have you. We can't bargain or bully our way out of it this time."

"Ic'abod come out of there," the Chief demanded. "That's an order."

"Sorry Chief, the time for orders is over. My time is over. Your time is over too, but you don't see it that way, not yet anyhow. I've enjoyed working with you, but its time to go."

With that last statement Ic'abod's hand punched the outer door release. In a moment all the air within the airlock was swept into outer space along with small particles of debris, a stray piece of paper and Ic'abod's body.

The Station Chief stared at the empty air lock for a long time. Muttering a silent curse he pressed a series of controls on the inner panel and cycled the outer door shut. As he walked away he continued to mumble half-silent epithets, an act that would become a habit in the days to come.

* * *

Vladian finished his weather report and transmitted it to all the stations that could receive his signal. While he waited for the Station Chief's return he examined the automatic logs for signs of military communication relay traffic between the surface and any receivers in deep space. There'd been very little after the Pentagon explosion and none at all in recent weeks. The stillness was eerie and very unusual. It didn't take a superstitious person to recognize the portent of greater disaster. The lack of comm traffic certainly qualified as one. Something more than leadership had died. Did Ic'abod know what it was? Was that why he'd become so despondent and slack with his duties? Vladian didn't know.

The Chief reappeared in the observation chamber somewhat less starched than usual. Vladian heard mumbling behind him and stood to his feet to acknowledge the Chief's arrival, "Is Ic'abod coming to relieve me?"

The Chief cleared his throat, "Ic'abod's dead. He cycled the outer door and blew himself into space. You and I are the only remaining crew aboard this station."

Vladian took the news stoically, "I knew he was down about something. I just assumed it had to do with the Leader's death. We were all terribly shocked when it happened. I'll never forget what I was doing when I heard the news. Ic'abod never told me how he felt about it."

"He didn't say anything to me either," the Chief said.

The rookie blamed himself, "I'm sorry I didn't understand his mood. Maybe I could have said or done something to help him. This…act of suicide…I don't understand."

"He was young and impressionable," the Chief said. "I liked his style when he first came aboard, but perhaps his emotional plummet after the Pentagon explosion was more complicated than I realized. I suppose we'll never know if we could've helped him."

A long uncomfortable silence echoed off the walls around them. Even the air seemed to acquire a melancholy sigh as it blew through the vents into the chamber. The tiny room seemed to swell to an impersonal size leaving the two men alone with their thoughts in the vast universe. Busy work that'd once turned hours into seconds was gone, replaced by a gnawing stillness and isolation that seemed to be almost tangible. It could be felt and breathed like a real thing.

Vladian tried to break the somber mood, "You told me earlier you'd received a message. Would it be inappropriate for me to ask what it was about?"

"Our supply shipment has been delayed," the Chief said. "We can't expect to receive any additional food or replacement parts for several weeks, perhaps longer."

"We're already on restricted rations, sir."

"I know that," the Chief replied. "Fortunately, the plants in our hydroponic section can provide enough air and food for us to survive for quite a long time. We won't eat as well as we've been accustomed to in the past, but we won't starve."

"I thought hydroponics was only a secondary food and air supply. Don't we need resupply from the ground to augment what we grow here?"

"Not any more. This station was originally designed for fifteen to twenty people. Our hydroponics can't support that many, but now that we're reduced to two people there's plenty to last us a long time. My concern is about other matters."

"What other matters, Chief?"

The older man paused to compose his thoughts and choose his next words, "If I was to make an educated guess about our future on this station I'd say additional rations might not be needed. Our duties here may soon be at an end. The Shundite attack we've been expecting may terminate our responsibilities before anyone in command on the ground does so."

"Has something changed?"

The Chief's voice lowered to a whisper as though there were more than two people aboard the station who might overhear his words.

"I've been monitoring civilian and commercial traffic as well as military channels," the Chief said. "The war is lost. There've been military and political reverses everywhere. On the day of the Pentagon explosion a battle was fought over the last planetary outpost. I believe our interceptors won the battle, but were forced to withdraw anyway. The reasons for their retreat are rather vague."

"I read a summary report about the battle. Ic'abod must have read it too. I just didn't know how bad things had become. Maybe Ic'abod did."

"There's more," the Chief said. "Following the death of the Leader and his senior staff a struggle for power arose among the surviving Generals and provincial Governors. Something of an unofficial civil war is now in progress. Nobody is in charge any more. Five hundred years of the Leaders' dynasty was swept away in a single hour. The Cydonian Empire has been defeated in space by our enemies and shattered on our own world by those who seek personal advantage.

The war is lost. The Empire we came here to serve no longer exists and the world we see today isn't the same as the one we left. The only thing that's unchanged is it's natural beauty."

Both men watched the planet on the video screen as it slowly turned below them. Water spilled out of Vladian's eyes. He wiped it away with the back of his hand, hoping the Chief hadn't noticed.

"It's a beautiful world isn't it Chief?"

"It's the best, Vladian."

Without another word the Chief turned and walked out of the observation chamber. Vladian thought the older man walked with a slight stoop he hadn't noticed before. The Chief's footsteps grew fainter as he retreated down the passageway toward the airlock. He looked like a beaten man. No longer carrying himself tall and proud, he disappeared from view around a corner.

When the Station Chief arrived at the airlock he was surprised at how friendly and peaceful it looked. He decided to go in and sit a while - in a place where he could cry and curse and not be heard. Ic'abod had been right. The time for orders was over.

* * *

Each crewman aboard Phobos Station had his own quarters, but Vladian began spending his sleep cycles in the observation chamber – the better able to monitor signal traffic. A few nights became a week and after a week or so his presence in the small room became a habit rather than a duty. No further military communications or queries emanated from the surface or deep space. For all intents and purposes military activity appeared to have ceased.

Automatic equipment aboard the station continued to record weather patterns on the surface and Vladian continued to compose and transmit reports twice a day. The duty had once been part of his daily routine, but now the simple repetitive task provided a comfort. It was something that was still normal, as if normal meant anything any more. The rookie hoped someone out there would receive his report and be comforted too, but he had no way of knowing if anyone else knew or cared.

Vladian and the Chief lost track of time and each other, which was itself unusual due to the confines of the small station. Had it been weeks or days since Ic'abod died? Neither of the last two crewmen counted or cared. When the Station Chief wasn't engaged in monitoring communications he spent his time in the airlock as Ic'abod had once done. Vladian haunted the observation chamber continually. Neither saw the other except when they visited the galley to fix something to eat.

The Chief made a personal appearance in the observation chamber one day. Vladian hadn't heard from him or seen him in what seemed ages – a situation that had become the new normal. Abandoning military protocol, Vladian turned in his chair instead of standing to his feet.

"Hello Chief. What can I do for you today?"

"I have some bad news."

The Chief's appearance took Vladian completely by surprise. Disheveled unwashed and carrying himself with a distinct slouch, the Chief slurred his words and mumbled between sentences. His uniform was wrinkled and stained as though he'd lived and slept in it for weeks.

"Is there any other kind of news these days," Vladian asked.

The Chief ignored the attempted sarcasm, "I've been monitoring civilian and corporate message traffic. Remind me to show you how to do that. You'll find it very interesting especially since the military channels all appear to be as dead as the Leader."

"Thanks Chief, I'd like that."

"Disturbing chatter is in the air suggesting unmanned enemy reconnaissance probes have been detected within our own solar system. These are recent sightings, by the way. No one seems to know if they were intercepted or if their transmissions were jammed before they reported to their base of operations. I sent a query to Command via a closed encrypted circuit asking if our home world is being targeted for some sort of enemy attack, but there's been no reply. It's like trying to talk to a stone wall. They won't respond to any communication at all."

"Perhaps negotiations for peace will be possible," Vladian hoped.

"Those opportunities evaporated long ago. Command steadfastly refused every overture for peace from our enemies. Silence prevails now. In the last few years not even demands for surrender have been received. I fear the inevitable conclusion of our long war is near. I don't think we'll have to wait long for its arrival."

"But sir, no enemy spacecraft has ever penetrated our defensive perimeter. Nothing at all has been sighted within range of our planetary interceptors. Surely our defenses are sufficient to repel any attack."

An awkward silence followed the rookies' naive appraisal of their planet's defenses.

"Unfortunately I don't share your optimistic appraisal," the Chief said. "As far as I know we have no adequate defenses at all – none. Those that might be useful are crippled by a lack of leadership focus and planning. There's no one really in charge down there – no one with the courage or authority to make decisions. The political situation is still stormy and incoherent."

The Chief paused and wiped his brow with a shaking hand, "If the Shundite Alliance has learned of the death of the Leader and the confusion that has settled over our military, they won't hesitate to attack. They'll throw everything they've got at us and I imagine that'll be quite a lot. It might be a good idea if you reviewed the emergency procedures for abandoning this station."

The rookie swallowed hard, "Yes, sir."

"You might want to take advantage of the little time that remains to us," the Chief reflected. "You might want to memorize the way our beautiful world looks today. If the war comes home to us the destruction our enemies will visit upon us will be total. You might want to remember it's grandeur...how it looks now...how it looked before the Shundite Alliance arrived. Take a few pictures while you're at it."

The Chief paused for one more look at the display of the planet below, "It's a beautiful world down there isn't it?"

The old man turned and shuffled painfully out of the observation chamber toward the airlock.

"Yes sir. It's the best," Vladian whispered.

Neither of the men aboard Phobos Station knew how close they were to the day of reckoning and how terrible its arrival would be for everyone.

* * *
- First Bombardment –

It happened two days later.

A red alert light above the control panel in the observation chamber began blinking. Somewhere in Phobos Station the harsh whine of the war claxon sounded. Vladian ran out of his small observation chamber to Main Control where larger versions of their surveillance equipment had been installed. Orbiting reconnaissance satellites relayed their signals to the control room displays and recorders allowing observers there to watch the whole gruesome spectacle on TV. When Vladian arrived in the room the attack was already in progress.

Arriving at night throughout the eastern hemisphere, the first wave of the Shundite bombardment struck Cydonian population centers from the southern highlands to the shores of the northern Borealis Ocean. The stations' video screens revealed clusters of sparkling lights in the darkness below. Numbering in the hundreds and thousands they blanketed half the planet. Viewed from space the impression was not unlike the appearance of a multitude of summer fireflies. On the ground the experience was quite different. Unlike their harmless namesake, Shundite fireflies delivered a lethal sting.

Each spot of light on the video displays represented a thermonuclear detonation. There were thousands of them. The average yield, or explosive force of a single explosion, would later be measured at between thirty and fifty megatons each. One megaton was equivalent to one million tons of standard high explosive. Cities disappeared instantly. Entire regions were devastated in minutes. Millions of people, unaware of the attack, died in their sleep.

Flashing alert lights awakened the Station Chief, who'd been sleeping in the soundproof airlock. He arrived in Main Control as the Shundite attack peaked.

"What's going on," he asked.

"The Shundite Alliance has been bombarding the dark side of the planet for nearly a half hour, Chief. Where have you been?"

"Sleeping in the airlock. It's very quiet in there. You can't hear all the squeaks and groans and buzzing noises from the machinery."

"You can't hear the alarms either," Vladian said. "I wouldn't worry about it, though. When the Alliance gets through with us there won't be anything left to be alarmed about."

"How bad is it?"

"It looks like the bombardment is nearly finished. At its peak our sensors counted two thousand three hundred seventy-nine detonations in the eastern hemisphere. It was furious. Now there are only a few low yield explosions here and there."

"Can you see anything? Did anything survive?"

"The sensors don't pick up anything except hot spots. Half the planet is burning. Maybe we'll be able to see something when dawn arrives down there."

"How about the western hemisphere? Did the Capital City get hit?"

"Not at all. It's very strange. The Capital and the entire western hemisphere is still in daylight. Nothing happened there. Do you think the Shundite Alliance is done with its attack?"

"Not at all. Not a bit," the Chief said. "My guess is that they're saving the western hemisphere for something special."

"What could be worse than this," Vladian asked.

"You and I watched the attack," the Chief said. "What do you think?"

At ground level near the twilight region where day gives way to night, nuclear explosions had been visible for miles. Those who witnessed the initial bombardment experienced the sound of a detonation as a sudden sharp report rather than a thunderclap. It was followed a second or two later by a sustained roar. The heat and concussion of each blast burned or destroyed everything for miles in all directions, but if a witness happened to be far enough away they would have seen the heavens boiling with colored fire.

In the first few seconds of its ignition uranium, burning much hotter than molten metal, blinded most observers with its intense yellow-white light. If witnesses shielded their eyes from the initial detonation, they sometimes saw a strange transparent purplish aura around the fireball - produced by the radiations of the bomb and its fission/fusion products. Moments later the fireball's heat would cause it to levitate above the ground like some hellish infernal god rising from the land it had just destroyed. Unwilling to reveal its naked hatred of all creation, each fireball cloaked itself in roiling clouds of dust until it resembled an expanding darkening mushroom cloud. Some who shielded their eyes from the nuclear fire saw the bones of their own hands when the X-Rays arrived. Most witnesses did not survive long enough to record their observations for posterity, of which there would be none.

In her home on the ridge overlooking Tempe Terra, Raene was completing preparations for a dinner party with a few intimate friends. Loneliness had been gnawing at her heart again and she'd hoped the companionship would cheer her mood. A shadow had fallen over her mind. A dull ache clutched her heart. An unreasonable fear grew more intense with each hour.

Husband Rodion had been forced to cut his vacation short when he was suddenly recalled to his excavation work in the east. She'd wept miserably when he left and had spent recent sleepless nights on her terrace. In her heart she felt a terrible conviction she'd never see him again. Rodion called when he arrived safely and promised he'd ask for time off very soon, but his safe travels and firm assurances did nothing to calm her misgivings. Something was very wrong.

As she carried a hot casserole dish across the kitchen, Raene's vision grew dim, her surroundings vague and unreal. Before her eyes appeared the vision of a black flower sprouting in the midst of a beautiful garden. It grew with unusual speed choking and strangling every other plant and herb. Larger it grew as it crushed trees and houses with its gigantic petals and poisoned everyone who breathed its scent. It grew so large it challenged the sun and sky with its size. In the shadow of the black flower, the flesh of thousands of dead bodies was consumed to the bone by its roots and stems. Somehow Raene knew one of those skeletons was familiar to her. She lost her grip on the dish she carried, spilling its contents onto the floor - shattering the precious heirloom she'd once valued so highly.

Raene's heart labored under a weight of sorrow she'd never known. Silent sobs choked her throat. A flood of tears burst from her eyes. She dropped heavily onto a chair knowing, yet not knowing why she wept. In vain she attempted to dry the unrelenting flood with a paper napkin from the table, but it soon became soggy torn and useless. Her guests would never arrive that night – being detained by a strange sickness that suddenly affected everyone.

On Raene's side of the planet, the Shundite Alliance prepared to unleash its doomsday weapon – an ecosphere killer of extraordinary size and immense destructive power. The worst was yet to come.

* * *

- Second Bombardment –

Brutal hurricane winds flashing with lightning and raining radioactive acid swirled in the upper atmosphere. Generated by the intense heat of thousands of thermonuclear blasts, the dark dusty cloud layer began to spread beyond the eastern hemisphere – blocking the sun and forever chilling the tormented ground below. Charred soil, shattered stone monuments, and wrecked buildings littered the obscured landscape. Toxic radioactive fumes filtered into every corner and crevice above and below ground killing any living thing that had survived blast and fire. Only scoured dead ground remained where thriving cities had existed a mere half-hour earlier.

Vladian couldn't see anything from Phobos Station. The entire eastern hemisphere had disappeared from view. Spreading radioactive clouds confused orbiting sensors and blocked visual observations. The Station Chief was desperately busy at the communication station trying to contact someone in authority on the surface either by radio or QC channels. Civilian frequencies were jammed and confused. Military channels were completely silent. Automatic channels yielded unspecified data. The Station Chief heard only the electronic equivalent of the Cydonian death rattle.

Destruction from the first half hour of the Shundite attack had been so extensive no estimation of the damage was possible. Despite the death of millions of people the Chief feared a second barrage was imminent. He wouldn't have to wait long before his fears would be realized. Shundite vengeance had only paused before delivering its ultimate blow.

Hours later the war claxon sounded for the last time. Keyed by an automatic system still functioning somewhere on the planet below it called the weary rookie and his Chief away from their survey of the damage suffered during the first attack. Rubbing his tired eyes, the Chief read Defense Command's alert. It would be the last communication Phobos Station would receive from the home world or its machinery.

"What's it say," Vladian asked.

"It's an automated distress signal. The fleet is being recalled to defend the planet."

"It's a little late for that isn't it," Vladian asked. "Is that supposed to be good news?"

"Ordinarily I'd say it is, but we've never encountered an attack of this size and ferocity. I fear there'll be nothing left to defend when they arrive, if they arrive at all. There'll be no one to rescue."

The Station Chief's words were prophetic beyond his imagination.

All warning lights and claxons electronically linked to control centers on the ground abruptly failed. Every communication link fell silent. Only the soft regular sigh of the ventilator fans could be heard throughout Phobos Station. The sudden silence was eerie and deafening.

Vladian checked the observation recorders to learn what had happened and received the shock of his life, "Chief, you need to see this."

Two final detonations served to expend the full rage and vengeance of the Shundite Alliance upon the home world of the Cydonian Star Empire. Never before had the stars witnessed the absolute destruction of an entire world. Never before had a planet died at the hand of an intelligent species. Never again would its beauty inspire anyone, for even the remnants of its loveliness would pass away in microseconds.

Vladian and the Chief watched as recording equipment replayed the detonation of two gargantuan thermonuclear explosions on the surface of the western hemisphere. Two bright flashes, each of them miles in diameter, appeared on the surface. The effect of the combined blasts was of sufficient power to vaporize most of the Cydonian atmosphere.

Each was so large the fireballs' own heat raised itself dozens of miles into the atmosphere. From space it looked as though perverse miniature stars had appeared on the planet and were burning its bones to dust. Each flash created a concussion wave so massive and powerful it was clearly visible from space. Each shock wave was of sufficient power and inertia to reduce more than half the planet's infrastructure to powder.

Vladian watched as the shockwave moved rapidly across the surface of his home world. It approached Tempe Terra and the ridge above it, pulverized everything in its path, and moved on. Although he couldn't see the house where he grew up he knew he'd witnessed its destruction as well as the death of his mother. Like the horror he watched, emotional pressure held tightly within burst upon him in all its fury. The shock was too much for the young rookie and he collapsed into a dead faint.

Swirling and boiling, glowing with a purplish gamma-ionized light, the expanding fireballs continued to rise. Each became burning mushroom clouds balanced on miles wide filthy stems of dust and debris. The fireballs rose into the sky propelled by irresistible hatred as much as burning uranium and plutonium. Huge toxic clouds of radioactive dust combined with spreading darkness from the east to blanket the entire planet.

Even the veteran Station Chief was overcome with the sight of destruction never visited upon any world in the universe. He vomited and fell into a chair. Every thing and every one he'd ever known was gone. Neither he nor Vladian would be able to eat for a week.

When both men recovered sufficiently to compose themselves for something approaching routine duty, they resumed the effort of assessing the damage to their home world. They thought they'd seen it all. They thought Shundite work was finished.

They hadn't and it wasn't.

* * *

- Third Bombardment –

All cultures adopt funeral traditions when the time comes to bury their dead. The end of the war between opposing star systems was no exception. Like handfuls of dirt tossed into an open grave to signify the end of life, the Shundite Alliance did something like it on a planetary scale. Following the final nuclear bursts that had killed Cydonia a fusillade of asteroids and meteors fell upon the dead planet.

Fiery trails of falling asteroids streaked across the cloud darkened sky before they impacted the ground. Some of them seemed to fall straight down while others cut through the sky on a horizontal course before they lost their momentum and plummeted to the surface. Thousands of craters were plowed into the ground – each one marking an asteroid or meteor impact. Megatons of debris were thrown into the clouds, accumulating additional poisonous waste in the already irradiated atmosphere. Smaller meteors exploded in the air adding their own particular style of pyrotechnics to the lightning that still persisted from one hemisphere to the other. Very little additional damage was done to the surface because most of it had been wiped clean already.

The plague of rocks falling from the sky, which had tormented the Cydonian civilization in its early days, had been the harbinger of its end.

The Chief punched an inquiry into the military observation computers and received a humbling answer.

"Ninety-three percent of the asteroid impacts fell on the eastern hemisphere as well as several thousand nuclear blasts ranging from thirty to fifty megatons each. Only two thermonuclear detonations were recorded in the west. The largest one fell in the Cydonia Mensa region and registered approximately five hundred megatons of explosive force. To say the smaller of the two fell near Utopia Planum would be an understatement of its power. Our instruments measured the last blast at between four hundred and four hundred fifty megatons."

"What does that mean," Vladian asked.

"Apart from destroying everything above ground, that amount of destructive power is sufficient to cover the entire planet with a radioactive cloud for several years. The bulk of the atmosphere has been blown into space. Without its' protection solar radiation will complete the work begun by the nukes. Surface temperatures and air pressure will plummet to levels that cannot sustain life in any future we can imagine. Lacking an atmosphere of protective thickness, our oceans and seas will freeze or simply dissipate into empty space. Our beautiful blue-green world will become a dead rock in space. Only broken bits of buildings and stone monuments will remain as evidence that anyone ever lived there."

* * *

Automatic systems on Phobos Station continued to operate for decades powered by the same nuclear energy that had destroyed the world they watched. Years later, when the global dust clouds finally settled, recording equipment would map a world that had assumed the hue of radioactive iron-oxide dust. A strange green aurora, seen only from space, would forever haunt the dead planet's night sky. No rescue of the crew would ever materialize. Eventually the power source for the equipment would fail and Phobos Station would join the fate of the planet it perpetually orbited. The last two inhabitants of a once great civilization would be imprisoned in an orbiting outpost - reluctant spectators of the death of what would come to be known by the rest of the universe as the Red Planet.

Chapter 15
TEARS FOR CYDONIA

The day of the Lord will come as a thief in the night, in which the heavens will pass away with a great noise, and the elements will melt with fervent heat; both the earth and the works that are in it will be burned up. - 2 Peter 3:10 KJV

Lament for a dead world.

Weep for the land. Gentle rain no longer quenches its thirst.
Weep for the sky. White feathery clouds dance there no more.
Weep for the sea. Her proud waves no longer surge to the shore.
Weep for Cydonia, betrayed by her children destroyed by their greed.

Her mountains and hills are laid waste. No greenery clothes her nakedness.
Her rivers are waterless – silent and vanished from their place.
Her marshes are parched and unmoving. Teeming life has ceased its struggle.
Weep for Cydonia. Her fields and valleys are dead and unfruitful.

Blue sunsets end each day, a perpetual reminder she once lived long ago.
Pink bloody skies color each day, an everlasting sign she died by fire.
Green auras cloak her night sky, an eerie signpost of war's harvest of death.
Weep for Cydonia. The chill of death has replaced her living warmth.

Her children sowed the wind and reaped the whirlwinds of annihilation.
Shattered remnants of her past lie like gravestones beneath the sun.
Cydonia gave her children a life they spurned for the ways of death.
She speaks not of life once nurtured, but whispers quietly how she died.

Weep for Cydonia. Dust devils dance on the planitia once green and alive.
Her children corrupted themselves and summoned ruin.
Weep for Cydonia. Even her ghosts have perished. She is altogether barren.
No eye can see and no ear can hear of the loveliness that was once Cydonia.

"It's a beautiful world isn't it Chief?"
"It's the best, Vladian."

She was once called the garden world of the universe. Today she floats in space – a dead thing of no use to anyone - except perhaps to those who tell tales of the deeds of her children.

Muriel Rukeyzer once wrote, *"The universe is full of stories, not atoms."*

This has been one of them.